ABERDEENSHIRE
FOLK
TALES

ABERDEENSHIRE FOLK TALES

GRACE BANKS &
SHEENA BLACKHALL

The
History
Press

The Maidenstone and Other Stories

Grace Banks and Sheena Blackhall

'Stories, like seeds, blow where the wind takes them, to take root and grow in the unlikeliest of places.'

Dedicated to the memory of
Stanley Robertson MUniv, and to all others in our
lives who have brought story and song alive for us.

First published 2013

The History Press
The Mill, Brimscombe Port
Stroud, Gloucestershire, GL5 2QG
www.thehistorypress.co.uk

British Library Cataloguing in Publication Data.
A catalogue record for this book is available from the British Library.

ISBN 978 0 7524 9758 7

Typesetting and origination by The History Press
Printed in Great Britain

CONTENTS

Foreword		7
To Begin …		9
1	HILL AND GLEN	11
	Blelack	11
	The Legend of the Maidenstone	16
	Auld Slorachs	20
	Knock Castle	26
	The Strange Coachman	29
	The Pupil	34
	Mary Elphinstone	41
2	THE LAND	47
	The Tattiebogle	47
	The Ballad of Gilderoy	53
	The Highwayman and the Orra Loon	54
	An Aul Beggarman	58
	The Gudeman o' Ballengeich	62
	Templar Thunder Hole	65
	The Rat, the Tree and the Dragon	68
	The Trick	69
3	CASTLES	77
	French Kate	77
	Alison Cross	81
	The Plague Castle	83
	The Smith of Kildrummy Castle	86

The Baron o' Braichlie 90

The Children of the Trough 92

The Tad-Losgann (The Toad-Frog) 95

The Laird o' Drum 98

Tifty's Annie 101

4 FORESTS, RIVERS AND WATER 106

The Key Pool 106

The Giant with the Three Golden Hairs, or,
 The Seely Cap 110

The Wizard Laird of Skene (1665–1724) 119

The Pedlar 124

The Reel o' Tullich 125

Auld Creuvie 131

The Kelpie Tale 136

5 COAST AND SEA 139

Smugglers of Collieston 139

The Curse of Forvie 145

The Knock Maitland Stane 150

The Lass from the Sea 151

Power fae Beyond the Grave 154

6 THE CITY 161

The Story of Benholm's Lodgings 161

The Astronomer from Aberdeen 165

The Slave who came from Aboyne 170

Alexander Hadden of Hadden Mill 174

Wee Aipplies an' Wee Orangies 176

Riddles Solved 186

Bibliography 187

FOREWORD

Every region of Scotland is rich in story lore, but none more so than the North-East. Interwoven with ballads and poetry, the stories of Aberdeenshire are about landscape, history, working lives, games, passions, the supernatural, the everyday, the tragic, the comic and the downright ridiculous. And they are all in this book.

But what a treasury such as this requires is storytellers to bring it to life. And here in Grace Banks and Sheena Blackhall we have two great voices, rooted in the community and relishing the verbal magic, humour and strangeness of their sources. Storytelling has come back with a whoosh because people recognise the magic of the live art, the connection it establishes between people and between a community, its heritage and its environment. The authors of *Aberdeenshire Folk Tales* are great storytellers. Their texts have been fashioned on the tongue and lips and now they are offering their rich heritage back for everyone to share and tell.

Gathering the stories of Aberdeenshire, as Hamish Henderson said of Scottish traditions, is like holding a pail under a waterfall. There could be a line of books behind this, and maybe there will be. However our two storytellers have picked well and what you get here is rich and rounded, while also whetting the appetite for more. Grace Banks and Sheena Blackhall are themselves a living continuation of these traditions and through them a world of people and of place is given voice.

Some of the experiences reflected in these tales may seem at first hand to belong to a different world from the one in which we now live. But then you realise that the places are still there and that the emotions are still our own. That reflects the truth that through technological and social change, we remain human beings connected with everyone that has gone before and that will come after. Moreover our passions and hopes and desires are shared across the world regardless of creed, race or colour. That is why in valuing what is local we are also being truly global.

Behind this book you can feel the inspiration of Aberdeenshire's great twentieth-century storyteller Stanley Robertson. Traveller, piper, scholar, fish gutter, singer and teacher. Stanley's storytelling abounded in humour and the uncanny, but is at heart an expression of compassion and wisdom garnered through many generations. He would be proud of what Sheena and Grace have done in this book, giving it his blessing as a handsel for the future. I cannot say better than that.

I know you will enjoy reading *Aberdeenshire Folk Tales* – remember also to pass on the stories.

Donald Smith,
Director, Scottish Storytelling Centre

To Begin...

When Sheena asked if we could write this book together, I was delighted! What a wonderful opportunity to put on paper so many of the wonderful stories that are part and parcel of my life.

For Sheena and I there is one man who has been very significant for both our journeys: Stanley Robertson. As traveller and storyteller, his generosity, his wealth of tales and songs told with a mixture of dry wit and sensitivity, has been a great influence and encouragement to us both.

Many of the stories retold here have his voice behind them, but with our own individuality and years of telling, they have been moulded and metamorphosed into our telling of what are timeless tales of wisdom and life.

For Sheena, many of her tales are her inheritance, passed down through family connections:

> From the age of five my mother's way of dealing with an adventurous child was to deposit her on Strachan's, my aunt's touring bus of the Ballater area. This was out-with the normal Deeside bus service in that it catered for tourists who wished to know the legends of the Deeside area. The bus drivers knew all the stories of the locality ... Whenever I retell the legends it recaptures the smell of diesel and rickety wheels.
>
> When I went to Aberdeen University to study for an M.Lit. I was given the task of choosing an area in which to research the way that Scots is transmitted across the generations. Naturally, I choose the area of my ancestors, that of Upper Deeside and Migvie. I discovered that in the space of two or three generations, Gaelic

was dropped in preference to Doric. A hundred years or so on, Doric is receding in favour of English in this locality. Because the legends come out of this past, I have deliberately inserted here and there speech quotes from the Legends of the Braes o' Mar, where the writer, J. Grant of Glen Gairn, puts Deeside Gaelic into the mouth of a local chieftain, Iain Dubh Farquharson. Legends are rooted in history ... for me they are a way of keeping faith with the ghosts of the past.

For me, my storytelling journey began at the feet of my mother, whose retelling of *The Hobbit* and *The Lord of the Rings* brought the Shire, Sam Gamgee and all the adventures alive in my bedroom at home. My father too would create stories during our long car journeys where the five of us were sardined in the back. It was there that we all learnt many songs that still remain to this day!

I can remember whispering stories to my brother and sister in bed in the dark ... tales were just waiting to be woven from the colourful threads that my young mind had squirreled away in my imagination. Coming to Aberdeen and having children of my own kept the story flame alive and gradually, with encouragement from Angela Halvorsen Bogo, née Knowles, Claire McNicol and Jackie Ross, I began to realise how much telling stories is just a natural part of who I am. Through my work, I am greatly privileged to have been able to hone and develop my storytelling, becoming acquainted with the rich depth of tales from this area of Scotland.

Finally we would like to acknowledge and thank my son Josh Banks for all the support and hours of painstaking editing that he has spent to ensure this collection of tales was readable.

We hope you'll enjoy the tales and have fun with my riddles woven throughout the book!

Grace Banks

1

HILL AND GLEN

BLELACK

When my aunt, Isobel Craib of Tullyoch Farm, Echt, married her second cousin, George Booth of Skene, she would say that a piece of her heart was left in her birthplace, as if Skene were on the far side of the moon. She taught me many things, but one thing in particular concerned the Hill o' Fare, and the burn there 'which ran reid for days eftir a terrible battle ... nae man nor beast could drink frae it.' County folk have long memories. To this place, the fairies were sent. To find how they took the flitting, read on ... – S.B

Blelack House lies 30 miles west of Aberdeen, near the village of Logie Coldstone, 3 miles north of the River Dee in Cromar, in the Grampian foothills. The name Blelack is an Anglicisation of

the Gaelic *Baile ailich* meaning 'village of the stone house'. The
Royal Deeside area was historically within the Earldom of Mar,
and the Blelack estate belonged to a branch of the powerful Clan
Gordon. Nearby there was a farm and a mill, both built of the local
pink granite.

The home of the wizard John Farquharson, known as 'the
Fairy Doctor', was said to be the farm of Carue in the Parish of
Coldstone. On this farm is a knoll known as 'the Fairy Knowe',
on the top of which is a hollow well known as 'the Seely Howe'
(Hollow of the Fairy Court). Here, the fairies met and stayed, and

were so friendly towards the wizard that they composed a song for him, a fragment of which remains:

Johnny, I lo'e ye, Johnny, I lo'e ye
Nine tunes in ae nicht will I come and see thee.

Some time before setting off to fight for Bonnie Prince Charlie in 1745, the rebel laird of Blelack, who lived near Carue, took umbrage at having such supernatural neighbours and decided to force the wizard to clear the glen of the Seely Court. The fairies, incensed, refused as his spell had failed to allocate them an alternative residence. John Farquharson soon rectified that, commanding them to flit to the Hill o' Fare, 17 miles away. Sadly, and none too kindly, the fairies moved, but not before uttering a curse:

Now we maun awa' to the cauld Hill o' Fare,
Or it will be mornin' e'er we get there;
But though girse and corn should grow in the air, John Farquharson
and his folk shall thrive nae mair.

However, once they arrived at the Hill o' Fare, the fairies disliked the place so much that they also cursed the rebel laird of Blelack, Charlie Gordon, for good measure:

Dool, dool to Blelack, And dool to Blelack's heir
For drivin' us frae the Seely Howe
To the cauld Hill o' Fare!

On 15 January 1746, Charles Gordon of Blelack joined the Jacobite army. One Sunday, the minister in the Logie Coldstone Kirk prayed to God to scatter the rebel army, whereupon Lady Blelack, with some choice words, retorted, 'How daur ye say that an my Charlie wi' them?'

Three hundred and fifty press-ganged men commanded by Stoneywood, Blelack and Stoneywood travelled the country from Midmar to Braemar, forcing some tenants to enlist and others to pay the war tax. When the Jacobite rebellion was quelled, Blelack House was razed; the fairies' curse came true. Farquharson the wizard suffered bad luck from the very day he cast the spirits out.

Why did the fairies loathe the Hill o' Fare? On 28 October 1562 the Battle of Corrichie was fought there between the new Earl of Moray, James Stuart, half-brother to Mary Queen of Scots and the 4th Earl of Huntly, George Gordon. The Battle of Corrichie is immortalised in an old ballad, of which there is a remnant below. It was first printed in the July 1772 edition of *The Scots Weekly Magazine*. It was reputed to have been written by Mr Forbes, schoolmaster at Maryculter, Deeside.

Murn, ye Heilans, and murn ye Lowlans, I trow ye hae muckle
    need;
For the bonnie burn o' Corrichie
Has run this day wi' bluid.

The hopefu' Laird o' Finliter
Earl Huntly's gallant son,
For the love he bore our beauteous queen, Has gar't fair Scotland
    moan.

The story here runs that Sir John Gordon, Laird of Findlater, one of the Catholic Earl of Huntly's sons, had fallen in love with Mary Queen of Scots and wished to marry her. The Gordons mustered 1,000 men, whereas James Stuart, who wished to block Gordon's power, led 1,300 cavalry. At the height of the battle, Gordon, who was of huge girth, rose in his stirrups in his heavy armour, suffered a heart attack and fell dead from his horse. Local Echt folk up to the twentieth century still recalled that the burn of Corrichie ran red for many days, so many were slaughtered on that hill. Huntly's son, the queen's would-be suitor, and other members of his family, were taken in chains to Aberdeen.

Five Gordon nobles were hanged there, but Lord John Gordon was condemned to be beheaded. The beautiful Mary Queen of Scots, who had watched the Battle of Corrichie, was forced to witness the execution from a window of the Earl Marischal's house on the south side of the Castlegate. The executioner was unskilled, and it took several strokes to kill the unfortunate man. Strathbogie Castle was then relieved of its contents, including the treasures from the Cathedral of Aberdeen. Silver and gold plate, jewellery, gorgeous textile fabrics and clothing were dispatched to the palace of Holyrood to adorn the hall of Kirk-o'-Field where Lord Darnley, Mary's second husband, had been murdered. The old ballad ends with wishes that were not granted in Mary's reign:

I wish our queen had better friens
I wish our country better peace
I wish our lords wid nae discord
I wish our wars at hame may cease

After Huntly's death, his body and possessions were transported from Strathbogie Castle to Edinburgh. It was brought to the Scottish Parliament on 29 May 1563, seven months after his death. There his coffin lid was opened and the coffin propped up so that the earl might hear the charges against him. The court ruled that the Gordon estates be forfeited. Huntly's body lay unburied in Holyrood Abbey for three years. After this, it was returned to Moray for burial at Elgin Cathedral. His valuables were taken to Holyrood Palace. When Mary was imprisoned at Loch Leven, she was given the earl's cloth-of-estate. As for the fairies, rumour has it that in more recent times a white witch built fairy houses throughout the Blelack estate in an attempt to encourage the little people back to their beloved Seely Howe.

THE LEGEND OF THE MAIDENSTONE

If you are passing by Bennachie, it is worth the time to go and see this magnificent standing stone, believed to be of Pictish origin. I have heard many versions of the tale, but this is my favourite. – G.B.

Mary loved to bake. For her, it was never a chore, no matter how many scones, bannocks or pancakes she had to turn out. She and her parents lived in a smallholding at the foot of Bennachie, where her father tended to his beasts.

Mary gazed south from the kitchen window, as she had done every day for the last two years, always hoping for the familiar sight of Sandy, her betrothed, to come striding across the fields. He had left penniless to join the army, vowing to return with wealth enough to marry his beloved. With a sigh, Mary went back to beating the pancakes; even her hopeful spirit could not remain optimistic when there had been no word of Sandy in all this time.

It was the following Sunday, when everyone was leaving the wee kirk, that Mary first caught sight of the stranger. He was leaning on the stone parapet of the bridge as she and her parents walked home; a striking figure, tall, and dressed in black. He was very handsome. As Mary passed, she glanced curiously at the man's face, and he smiled at her with a look in his dark eyes that made the lass's legs falter and her belly tighten.

All through that week, whenever her thoughts drifted back to the handsome, dark stranger, her heart would skip a beat, and a smile play on her lips.

When Sunday came around once more, the lass dressed with particular care, and carefully set her hair in becoming ringlets. Sure enough, when the crowd emerged from church, there was the stranger, only this time he was standing beneath the ash tree, close by the kirk. He moved out of the shade as Mary's father passed by. 'Good day, sir,' he said, his voice mellow and warm.

Her father looked up at the tall man. 'Aye, good day tae ye. You were no in the kirk.'

'The likes is no for me, but I wis wondering if I might walk yer daughter hame?'

Mary had been standing behind her father, longing to look up into the stranger's face again, yet fearful to do so. But now, startled at his enquiry, her eyes met his, and she suddenly felt giddy. The man smiled at the lass. She blushed and, looking flustered, stared down at her feet.

Mary's father, seeing this exchange, cleared his throat. 'Aye, ye can walk Mary up the road, but tell me stranger, fit's yer name an far d'ye come fae?'

'Ma name, sir, is Mr Black, an I hiv recently arrived to settle frae doon sooth. I own land on the other side o' the hill.' Mary's father nodded. 'Aye, very well then.' He turned to his daughter. 'Noo, Mary, we'll see ye back at the hoose.'

'Aye, Faither,' she said quietly, her heart thumping loudly in her chest. Then, lifting her head, she looked again into the man's eyes and smiled. He smiled back.

'Mary, shall we walk?' he asked merrily, and held out his arm. Trembling, the lass placed her small hand through his arm, and suddenly felt happy.

From that day onward, Mr Black would be waiting for Mary each Sunday, and as she went about her daily work, her steps were light, and there was always a song on her lips. Her parents were pleased for their daughter, and when one day she came home wearing a lovely gold bracelet, set with rich red rubies, they looked at each other with a smile.

A few months later, Mr Black spoke with Mary's father privately, and the following week, there was great happiness in the little home as Mary joyfully brought her betrothed in for Sunday dinner with a beautiful ring on her wedding finger.

There was merry chat around the table as Mary and her mother brought through steaming bowls of soup. Later, as Mary's father was cutting the meat, he accidentally dropped the knife, and reached under the table to retrieve it. When he sat up again, his face was pale.

'Faither, are ye well?' cried Mary.

'Ach, I'm nae richt. Can ye jist tak me ootside a wee minute?' Mary stood up, and alarmed, helped her father out of the door.

When they were out in the sunshine, Mary's father breathed deeply and turned to look at his daughter with troubled eyes.

'Ye canna mairry that man, lass.'

'Faither? Fit's wrang?'

'He's nae a man; it's the deil himsel! Fan I wis under the table, I saw he hisnae ony feet, but cloven hooves! It's Clovenhoddie!'

Mary's face turned ashen, and her head suddenly felt painful. There was a crunch behind father and daughter, and there stood Mr Black, looking concerned. 'Mary? My love, are you well?' He reached out to clasp her waist, but she moved away to the safety of her father's arms, who gazed fixedly at the tall man before him.

'Bide awa' fae ma daughter,' he said quietly, 'she's nae fer the likes o' you.'

Mr Black smiled, but there was no warmth in it. 'Ah, but that's where yer wrang. Mary his promised tae mairry me, an sae she is mine.'

'I winna mairry ye. Yer nae a man at a'!' Mary cried, and burst into tears, her heart full of fear and disappointment.

The devil looked sadly upon the distressed lass, and said gently, 'Mary, is that how ye really feel?' Mary nodded, not daring to look up into his dark eyes. 'Weel, because you are sae dear tae me, I will gie ye a chance tae be freed frae oor betrothal. Tomorrow at first licht, I will build a road frae the top o' Bennachie doon tae here, an if ye can mak one hundred bannocks afore I complete it, then ye'll be free an I will leave ye alane.'

Mary, her face buried in her father's shoulder, was suddenly still, but her mind was racing. Surely that would be easy? She was such a deft hand at baking. Slowly, she nodded her consent, and the tall man left without another word.

As the first rays of sun filled the dawn sky with a pinkish pearly light, the kitchen fire was already glowing bright, and Mary had the first batch of bannocks ready for firing on the griddle.

She worked with a will, her parents silently encouraging her, their tension showing as they moved from the kitchen to the front door to gaze up at the brow of Bennachie. Even as they watched, a white streak appeared, and began to extend down the hill, slowly but inexorably creeping closer.

Feverishly, Mary's hands flew and the pile of baking grew. She glanced at her mother, her brown hair dishevelled, the smell of bannocks rich in the air. The mother smiled confidently at her daughter. 'Yer doin' grand, lass. He's nae that close yet. How mony hiv ye baked?'

'Eighty, Mither.'

'Another batch then?'

'Aye, een mair shid dee.' Carefully, deftly, Mary fired the next batch – 85 ... 89 ... 92 ... 94 ...

'Mary?'

Startled, she looked up, and there, standing at the back door, was a broad shouldered man, thinner and older than she remembered, but still the strong kind face that she knew. Time seemed to stop, and then as if she had suddenly awakened, Mary cried, 'Sandy!'

Her hand faltered, and the bowl with the remaining bannock mix fell to the ground, spilling onto the flagstoned floor.

With a cry of despair, Mary reached down, but even as she did, she heard a moan escape her mother's lips. Terrified, she looked up to see the dreaded figure darkening the front door.

Pushing past her dear and bewildered Sandy, Mary ran, but even as she did, the devil called to her, 'No, Mary.' She felt an iron-cold grip on her shoulder, and that was the last she ever knew. The ring fell from the lass's petrified finger and became a toad that hopped away; the bracelet slipped from her wrist and turned into a small snake that slithered away into the long grass. In a whiff of sulphur, the devil vanished.

If you look at the Maidenstone today, you will see that it is all that remains of Mary. There is a crack near the top on the right side where the devil placed his cruel hand on her shoulder, and at the base, the lass's mirror and comb are still on view for all to see.

Auld Slorachs

When Stanley Robertson and I were guests of the Smithsonian Institute in Washington, an incident nearly cut short his career rather dramatically. We were chatting in the mall when a shot rang out, and the cup of water he held in his hand exploded into pieces.

'They surely dinna like traivellers here, either,' he responded.

We adjourned to the relative safety of the trees to sing to each other, by way of passing the time. I began by singing 'Dark Lochnagar', one of my father's favourites:

Away, ye gay landscapes, ye gardens of roses,
In you let the minions of luxury rove,
Restore me the rocks where the snowflake reposes

Though still they are sacred to freedom and love.
Hail Caledonia, belov'd are thy mountains,
Round their white summits the elements war,
Though cataracts foam 'stead of smooth-flowing fountains
I sigh for the valley of dark Lochnagar.

'I ken a story aboot the white summit o' Lochnagar,' Stanley interjected. 'Traivellers thocht it wis the white semmit (vest) o' Lochnagar, an they tell a story aboot it …'

And so he told it. In the tale, he said that the young hero took advice from 'a wise man', and the wisest man in Upper Deeside at one time was Neddy Broon, the Tarland wizard:

You'll find as good as e'er drew blood
Tae fecht in Tarland town, man
Knock down their foes wi' hearty blows
And nobly thump their crown, man

They needna come here frae Strathdon
Tae brag, and dare Cromar, man
Our Deeside boys make little noise
They ken our Tarland laws, man

They needna come to try our hand
At clubs, or shak o' faas, man
The Leochel men may keep their glen
Among the frost and snaa, man
If they come here, we'll gie them cheer
And chase them far awa, man

That is an English version of the Tarland Laws, a clachan feared all the length of the Dee and the Don for its fearsome warlike nature and the fact that its men are quick to outwit any enemies. I can personally vouch for the truth of this, for my own grandfather was a Tarland Tyke, and would stand at the market cross on fair days threatening to fight all comers. It was just as well for a farm servant called Jockie, who happened to live and work in Cromar, that he was possessed of the warlike nature of the area. Here, via Washington, with a nod to Tarland, is 'Auld Slorachs'.– S.B.

Now it happened that Jockie was friendly with one of the wisest men in the area, the Wizard of Tarland, Neddy Brown. Neddy's power was legendary. At one fair, he drove gypsies from the field with a swarm of bees, conjured out of a pile of grated cheese. He could freeze horses in the stable, turn millwheels backwards, cause pale blue lights to dance along the Howe, and ghosts to fly up over dykes and hills.

Jockie had worked in Cromar since he'd been a boy of seven, first as a cowherd, later undertaking all the work needed in one of the richest grounds in the area, 'the breadbasket of Mar'. He had a temper, did Jockie, but he'd learned how to control it, by diddling … 'Dee doo dee dree drum dree,' he would mutter to stop himself exploding.

Every month, he visited his old mother in Tullich, who scratched out a living there as a henwife. Being a dutiful and kind son, he gave her money to help out. This went on till Jockie was twenty-one years old, when he went to his mother's hut one day and found her in tears.

'Laddie, laddie,' she cried, 'The laird has raised my rent! If I pay what he's asking, I'll have nothing left for food.'

'Dee doo dee dree drum dree,' muttered Jockie, 'Dee doo dee dree drum dree!'

Striding up the road, he set off for the laird's house to confront him. The laird was normally a fair man, so Jockie was prepared to hear his reasoning behind such a cruel action. The laird was quick to share the problem. A powerful wizard had moved into the area, Auld Slorachs. He was one of the old Druidic breed, a Pict, with his grey hair pulled back and tied like a pony's tail, and he travelled everywhere on a piebald horse. He had kidnapped the chief's only daughter, Jeanickie, and was holding her to ransom. Every month, the laird must pay a huge ransom, or the girl would be killed.

'Leave it with me,' said Jockie. 'I'll speak with a wise man who might have an answer to this.'

Jockie returned to Cromar and went in search of his friend Neddy Brown. As he had hoped, the Tarland wizard quickly came up with a plan. The following Monday, Auld Slorachs appeared at the laird's house for his ransom money, and Jockie was waiting for him.

'So you are the powerful wizard the whole country is talking about?' he said.

Auld Slorach never shifted a foot from the stirrup, but smiled and nodded wickedly.

'I'm here to issue a challenge, your magic pitted against mine,' cried Jockie. 'If you can make all the snow melt from the summit of Lochnagar in three days, I'll be your servant for life and the Devil, your master, is welcome to keep my soul. Ay, and that's the snow of the Cuidhe Crom too, that hardly melts ever. But if you fail, mind, and with my magic I stop you winning, you will release young Jeanickie and never trouble the good folk here again.'

The great wizard was proud as well as powerful. He was sure he could crush the boy's magic as easily as cracking a nut. He leapt from the saddle and fixed his gaze on the summit of Lochnagar and the small corrie of snow beside it. From his saddlebag, he drew out three strands of wool, red, blue and white in colour, and nine feathers. Two of the feathers, black and white, were from the tail of a rooster, symbol of the horned god, both curved like horns. Another seven feathers he selected, all with different powers and symbolic meanings, and these he began to weave into the strands of wool, making a magic rope, or witch's ladder. As he wove, he cried aloud this charm:

> Yarn of red and black and white
> Work your magic spell this night
> With this feather and this string
> Power to me this charm will bring.

When he was done, he joined the ends together to make a complete circle, and stepping inside it, he raised his hands to Lochnagar and cried:

> In the names of the Goddesses and the God
> By Air, Earth, Fire and Water
> I consecrate this charm.
> Feathers nine and cord of three
> As I will, so must it be!

To everyone's amazement, the snow melted. Auld Slorachs was about to claim Jockie as his servant when the boy reminded him that the snow must stay melted for three days. The wizard laughed, and rode off, promising to return on the second day to prove his magic held good. Jockie left as soon as the wizard disappeared with his horse and cart.

'He's given up,' the laird announced, heartbroken. 'But what could a mere boy do against the power of a mighty druid wizard?'

The next day, however, when the sun rose in the sky, there, unmistakably, in the corrie near the summit of Lochnagar, was a small patch of white.

'The snow has returned!' everyone cried. 'Jockie's magic is beating that of Auld Slorachs!'

Auld Slorachs appeared again on his piebald horse, and again he drew from his saddlebag three strands of wool, red, blue and white in colour, and nine feathers. As before, two of the feathers were from the tail of a rooster, again black and white. Again, he took up the other seven feathers, and these he began to weave into the strands of wool, making a magic rope. As he wove, again he repeated this charm:

Yarn of red and black and white
Work your magic spell this night
With this feather and this string
Power to me this charm will bring.

When he was done, he joined the ends together to make a complete circle, and stepping inside it, he raised his hands to Lochnagar and cried:

In the names of the Goddesses and the God
By Air, Earth, Fire and Water
I consecrate this charm.
Feathers nine and cord of three
As I will, so must it be!

This time the snow did not melt.
Jockie held a yellow parchment with the following words on it:

Ad articulorum dolorem
Constantem Malignantium
Diabolus ligauit
Angelus curauit
Dominus saluauit
In nomine medicina

Taking a lit candle, he set fire to the corner, and waved the paper before Auld Slorachs.

'Tomorrow is the third day,' he warned him. And away he drove again on his horse and cart.

On the third and final day, the patch of snow had grown even bigger. Auld Slorachs' power was exhausted. Drained of his magic, he was defenceless, and had to admit defeat. Word was sent to the Wizard of Tarland, Neddy Brown, who came down from Cromar, and turned him into a stone, which was sent to the church at Migvie. From that day to this, Auld Slorachs stands in the old kirkyard there, a Christian cross at his back to keep him tethered.

But you'll be wondering what powerful magic Jockie used to keep the snow on the summit of Lochnagar from melting? Well, every night when he left the glen in his cart and horse, he filled the cart to the brim with salt, and drove it up to the very top of the mountain, over back roads and heather paths. So it wasn't the snow that defeated the power of Auld Slorachs, it was salt, which, as everyone knows, can blind the very Devil himself.

And what was the spell that Jockie burned on the paper? Why, a simple cure for rheumatism, as any apprentice witch or wizard could tell you!

Riddle One

Lazily I see you turn
You lie-a-bed!
Yet I've seen how fast you run!

KNOCK CASTLE

Every summer till I was sixteen, we stayed in Ballater, where my father worked. As I was a 'raikin aboot vratch', always pestering him to take me up Glen Muick, he bought me a bike, and the odd thing was I always stopped to rest at Mill o' Sterin. For some incomprehensible reason, I felt a strong psychic pull to the place.

When I was fifty, I answered the door to find a Tarland man standing there. 'Can I come in?' he asked, adding, 'Ye'd better sit doon.'

Once seated, he told me I had an older half-brother in Canada; his father, Charles Middleton Ritchie. I learned that my father had an affair as a young man with a Ritchie girl, and my half-brother was the result. His mother sailed off to Newfoundland, and left him behind with her parents and sisters to bring up. When we eventually met, it was very emotional, the more so when he told me his happiest childhood days were spent at the farm of Mill o' Sterin with his aunt Connie Fraser. How often I must have passed my brother's door!

In the brief time we shared together before he died, we discovered we both knew the legend of Strathgirnoch, he from his grandparents, and myself from 'The Legends of the Braes o' Mar' by John Grant. Both of us thought it chilling. Read it and judge for yourself. – S.B.

Knock Castle is a ruin of four storeys, located on the top of a grassy hill to the west of the ancient Brig o' Muick. The word knock comes from the Gaelic *cnoc*, a knoll, which afforded the Gordons a commanding view of the area. The building stands on a road that goes on to pass Abergeldie Castle, and carries on up to Balmoral. The first floor contained the Castle hall, and there was also an enclosed courtyard and a vaulted basement. The actual tower was erected in 1600, but the tale of the Gordon-Forbes feud began several years earlier. Harry Gordon of Knock and 'Black' Arthur Forbes of Strathgirnock had a disagreement after the battle of Corrichie in 1562.

Strathgirnock today is a beautiful, peaceful place; a small glen that lies between the tangy forests of Creag Phiobaidh and Creag Ghiubhais. There is no trace remaining of the old mansion house of Strathgirnock, which stood in the lee of Creag Phiobaidh, having been torched by the Gordons.

Old legends tell that Black Arthur bridged the Girnock burn with a stone so huge that four Gordons were unable to shift it. The Gordons were so incensed by this affront that one night they drove off all of Strathgirnock's cattle in revenge. In retaliation, a weaver called Muckle Fleeman rustled Harry Gordon's cattle and held them hidden till the Gordons returned the beasts they had originally stolen.

Harry Gordon was killed by Clan Chattan in 1592, and it was suspected that Black Arthur had a hand in this. In response, the Gordons of Auchindoun slaughtered all his servants and burned his mansion. Forbes himself escaped and went into hiding, relying on the loyalty and kindness of his tenants. A year later, the Gordons nearly apprehended him at Loinchork.

Now, Harry Gordon's heir was his brother, Alister. Alister had eight sons, and the most handsome of these, a lad called Francie,

fell in love with Black Arthur's only daughter. It was decided to send the Baron of Braichlie, who was well respected in the area, to plead the boy's cause, but rashly, Francie, with a lover's zeal, decided to cut out the middleman and approach Black Arthur himself. Black Arthur raised his sword, intending to scare the boy away, but the scabbard flew off and the unfortunate Francie was decapitated, his head rolling off on the grass like a ball.

Gordon of Auchindoun interceded on his kinsman's behalf and imprisoned Black Arthur for more than a year. When he was finally released he returned to Strathgirnock to find that the Gordons had dispossessed him. The Gordon's seven remaining sons had been given his lands, and were cutting peats there. Black Arthur rode furiously down the field, slicing off each boy's head as his horse caught up with them. He then collected his gruesome trophies and impaled them on top of their peat spades, set up like a row of coconuts in a fair.

One of the Gordons' servants came to the moor with lunch for the young men, but seeing the horrific sight, he fled screaming back up to the Knock with the news. Gordon, hearing that all of his sons had been killed, is said to have suffered a heart attack, toppling over his stairway down to his death. His kinsmen, the Abergeldie Gordons, like the hornets' nest that they were, swarmed out and captured Black Arthur. He was hanged, along with his tenant Wattie McRory, from a nearby tree. Thereafter Abergeldie claimed the lands of Strathgirnock and Knock for himself. It is said that the ghost of Gordon of Knock haunts the ruins of the castle to this very day.

The Strange Coachman

This story was related to me by Stanley Robertson. He told me that the Pass of Ballater was a favourite camping spot with the travellers, as it was sheltered, near the village, with fresh running water. Around that time, he taught me one of his mother's songs, describing the hard life of the travellers, which I have included. It's interesting, as the tune he sang it to is an old Gaelic Glen Gairn air, about the weary job of clearing bracken. Glen Gairn is the nearest glen to the pass, and so I have given this as the supernatural coachman's route. I have often stayed in a caravan at Glen Gairn at the Prony, but as a holidaymaker, not a traveller. It is a beautiful, secluded glen, where trout are plentiful. My father told me that one local farmer regularly tossed a stick of dynamite into a pool there, and then collected the stunned fish by the basketful. Many legends are associated with this place, one of the last Gaelic speaking areas in Aberdeenshire. – S.B.

A Tinker Woman's Lament – To the tune of 'Puin Bracken' (Tha mi Sgith).

Some of the words in the song are from the Cant language:

My hands are sae sair, maakin besoms, maakin besoms
My hands are sae sair aa' wi' maakin besoms
Maakin besoms aa day lang, aa' wi' maakin besoms
Maakin besoms aa day lang, aa' wi' maakin besoms.

My legs are scadded raw, hawkin hooses, hawkin hooses
My legs are scadded raw, aa' wi' hawkin hooses
Hawkin hooses aa day lang, aa' wi' hawkin hooses
Hawkin hooses aa day lang, aa' wi' hawkin hooses.

My back's bent an booed, cookin habin, cookin habin
My back's bent an booed, aa' wi' cookin habin
Cookin habin aa day lang, aa' wi' cookin habin
Cookin habin aa day lang, aa' wi' cookin habin.

My heid's throbbin thrawn, pingin kenchins, pingin kenchins
My heid's throbbin thrawn, aa' wi' pingin kenchins
Pingin kenchins aa day lang, aa' wi' pingin kenchins
Pingin kenchins aa day lang, aa' wi' pingin kenchins.

My sowel is perjured sair, tellin fortunes, tellin fortunes
My sowel is perjured sair, aa' wi' tellin fortunes
Tellin fortunes aa day lang, aa' wi' tellin fortunes
Tellin fortunes aa day lang, aa' wi' tellin fortunes.

When I'm deid and in my grave, I'll fin peace and I'll fin rest
When I'm deid and in my grave, then I'll fin my rest
Then I'll tak a lang, lang sleep, then I'll get my rest
Then I'll tak a lang, lang sleep, then I'll get my rest!

A favourite over-wintering campsite for the Deeside travelling folk
was the Pass o' Ballater, around three quarters of a mile from the
village. The road through the pass runs from Milton of Tullich to
the Bridge of Gairn, about 2 miles in length, and passes between
the oak woods of Craigendarroch (hill of the oaks), which rises to
1,250ft on the left, and Creag an t-Seabhaig (Cliff of the Falcon)
on the right. Once, there was a silver mine in the pass; now
there is only the ghost of the Black Colonel, and he only appears
now and then, and only to folk he takes a dislike to. Near the
Bridge of Gairn, the pass joins the main road between Ballater
and Braemar.

The travellers used to pitch their bow tents between those two
hills, and set to work earning a living as tinsmiths, horse dealers,
and hawkers. Some groups made bow tents from flexible wood,
ash or hazel saplings, called gellys. In the winter, the frames
were stronger and thrust deeper into the ground, as a defence
against blizzards. They were covered with thick coarse canvas,
or waterproof sheeting, with straw on the ground. A well-built
bowie could hold seven of a family easily; girls on one side, boys
at the foot, parents on the other side and a stove in the middle.
But other travellers preferred gypsy-style hooped caravans, and one
family in particular liked to camp at the pass in the *Evening Star*, a
fine wooden caravan pulled by a white jennet named Pinto. They
travelled alone as a family, with their hound Joukil as a faithful
guard dog. Often scaldies, or non-travellers, torment the travelling
folk, so a dog is a good companion to have.

One winter, a traveller youngster was sent out 'dry hunting', earning money by offering his labour around the countryside. His name was Jeemsie. He set off very early, working his way to the top of Glen Gairn from the pass. It was a crisp, cold day. He had worked up at Loch Builig in the afternoon helping an old shepherd, but now he was tired and keen to get back to the *Evening Star*. He had earned two white hares from the shepherd, some butter and turnips, and a pocketful of coins from crofters along the glen, chopping sticks for folk, or feeding animals. It was a long way back, and the sky was beginning to darken. He was starting to wish he hadn't gone so far up the glen, especially as the weather was so changeable, when through the dusk he could just make out an old fashioned post coach drawn by four black horses.

To his surprise, the coachman cried 'Whoa!' and the horses stopped. His face was hidden by a large, black, slouching hat, and his mouth was muffled by a scarf. He was a smartly-dressed man, and well spoken.

'Would you like to jump up on the seat beside me, laddie?' he asked. 'I've a couple of stops to make further down the glen, and some passengers to take on board yet, so I can't offer you an inside perch.'

The first flakes of thick snow had begun to fall from the sky, and the moon had a milky ring round it, a sure sign that a storm was coming. The coach stopped first at Gairnshiel, 5 miles up the glen. There are belts of larch trees there, but the lower slopes of the hills are covered with birch, alder, and groups of Scots pine, rowan and aspen trees. Amongst the trees, where bare branches were beginning to wear a layer of snow, was a small hut where a gamekeeper lived. The coachman handed the reins to Jeemsie and trudged up the hill to the hut. He returned with his passenger, a man dressed all in white, who spoke not a word nor looked once at Jeemsie before stepping into the coach. Off they went again, the snow flurries continuing to fall, and, if anything, growing thicker.

The second stop was a mile further along, near the burial ground of the Macdonalds of Rineaton, set on rising ground. It was about half an acre in size, encircled by a stone wall and surrounded by larch trees. The Macdonalds of Rineaton are descended from the Lord of the Isles. The first Macdonald of Rineaton was taken prisoner at the Battle of Harlaw, and not long after that the Earl of Mar granted to him the lands of Rineaton. The coachman again handed the reins to Jeemsie, and he set off to collect his strange passengers from an old mansion house near the kirkyard. This time, two people came out; a young woman with a newborn baby in her arms, both of them mute as stones, and dressed in white.

After he had settled them inside the coach, the strange coachman leapt up onto the driving seat, took back the reins and with a soft 'Hup', he encouraged the horses to trot on. They rode on until they were within 2 miles of the Brig o' Gairn, at the ruined Catholic chapel and the burial ground of Dalfad. The tombstones here mark the graves of the Glen Gairn MacGregors. Twenty-four of them gathered in the glen, and marched to Culloden where eighteen of their number were killed. The Lord of Aboyne had written to everyone in the glen threatening to burn their homes down around their ears if they refused to fight for Prince Charlie, but the MacGregors were Jacobite by inclination. There was only one old MacGregor left now, a hen wife living near there in a house thatched with heather and turf, half-buried in the moor. Surely she couldn't afford to travel anywhere by coach, thought Jeemsie.

This time, when the coachman stepped down and handed Jeemsie the reins, he waited till the man was a little way off, and jumped down himself. He tethered the horses to a tree, and followed the coachman right up to the hen wife's door. He watched him enter the house, and crept up to the tiny window to see what would happen next. Inside the house, the old hen wife lay stretched out on her bed, completely still, her eyes frozen and fixed in her head. With a shudder, Jeemsie noticed that her nails were black, where the blood had ceased to flow. The coachman looked down upon her, and light poured from his palms onto the corpse. Up from the body rose her spirit, dressed all in white; a pure and clean soul that had not long ago shed its fleshly cage.

'The Angel o' Daith!' gasped Jeemsie, knowing that there was still room on the coachman's seat for another passenger, if that passenger was a small one.

He fled down the hill, half tumbling, half sliding, taking shortcuts over the snowy hills the coach could not drive over, not stopping till he reached the pass. There, at the foot of Craigendarroch, was a strange, red, angry glow … the *Evening Star* was alight and burning, and his family with it. Sobbing and wailing, his heart hammering so hard it was like to fly out of his ribs, he rushed towards the inferno. Imagine his joy to find them cowering under the trees, but safe!

'Faither, Mither!' he cried. 'Thank God the Angel o' Daith has spared ye.'

'No, laddie, he never leaves a place empty-handed. Is onything missin?'

Jeemsie looked around, puzzled … and then he noticed that his dog Joukil was missing. Joukil, the faithful companion, who guarded the caravan and everyone in it, had perished in the flames, but not before waking them, and so saving their lives.

Riddle Two

The land that was bare
Now full of colour and life
Beauty and strife

THE PUPIL

So often men and women have been forced to prove their worth, not least to themselves, and for Hamish, it was no different. This story is Japanese in origin, and has been adapted in this instance to a Scottish setting. – G.B.

He had heard tell about a competition of strength to be held that winter in the village, and he was determined that he would win.

He was very capable, let there be no doubt, but it was because he bragged about it that others found cause to dislike this young man, and perhaps choose to walk the other way if they saw him coming.

The morning dawned bitter cold and frosty, and the ground was hard as stone. As Hamish unravelled himself from within his plaid, he breathed deep of the freezing air and watched with satisfaction as his breath billowed out in a large cloud from the depth of his mighty lungs. He was no small man!

Hamish found a small burn, well iced over. With his meaty fist, he smashed down until it shattered and, with skin like leather, cupped the icy water in his hand, raised it to his lips and swallowed greedily.

From a pouch at his waist, he drew out a handful of oatmeal, and mixed it with a little water in a small pot. He made a fire, and soon had his porridge cooking.

Hamish looked upward to see what weather he might encounter on his travels. The sky was just brightening; hazy with high cloud, while the sun shone through weakly with no warmth. Hamish believed he did not need heat; his massive frame kept him from feeling the cold, or so he thought. He relished this exposure as a test of his own strength, and the big-headed fool sighed with happiness when he reflected on his own wonderful example of a near-perfect male physique.

After his simple meal, Hamish surveyed the journey, which, for the next few days, would take him over hill and moor to reach his destination, the village of Tarland. There he would again prove his superior strength and endurance to all present. That self-satisfied smile played across his grudgingly handsome features once more.

Hamish set off directly, climbing for most of the morning. He had not travelled in this remote area before, and he was surprised when he came across a small glen in which was a fine stone holding with carefully cultivated land round about. Intrigued, Hamish began to clamber down a very steep path, which meandered up and down hills before entering the valley.

Suddenly, a figure hopped onto the path ahead of him. It was a young, healthy-looking lass, with a scarf twined round unruly red curls. She heard a sound behind her and turned. Hamish took a sharp intake of breath – what a lassie! Milk white skin, a tip tilted nose sprinkled with a few pretty freckles and bright rosebud lips that curved upwards in a beautiful smile as she saw the man behind her.

She turned and tripped lightly down the hill, carrying a large bucket of water in one hand. Hamish could not resist the opportunity. He swiftly caught up with the lass, reached out and tickled her slight but sturdy waist.

The lass let out a wonderful tinkling laugh. 'Oh you cheeky man!' she cried, and glanced round at Hamish with merry eyes. Encouraged, Hamish did it again. But as he did, the lass clamped her arm down in a vice-like grip on top of his thick wrist. Hamish pulled to release himself, but found that the lass had him held very tightly.

'You'd better let me go, lassie,' he said, concerned, 'I dinna want tae hurt you!' That tinkling laughter filled the air again. 'You wilna hurt me!'

Hamish strained harder, but still could not free himself. He tugged in vain, using his full strength, but, to his dismay and embarrassment, found the lass was still climbing the path at exactly the same pace, with him being dragged along behind! 'I beg ye, stop!' he pleaded. 'This is mortifyin!'

At once the girl stopped, but did not release her hold. 'Young man,' she said seriously, 'I suppose that you are headin to Tarland for the competitions?'

'Aye, I am that,' mumbled Hamish.

'And I suppose you presume to win?'

'Well … until now I did.'

'But the competitions are no' for another month. Why are you goin' so early?'

Hamish bowed his head and did not answer.

'Ah, I see! You were goin' to be at the inn every night, flexing your muscles and braggin', is that it?'

Hamish said nothing. That had been his plan, but now he had been humiliated by this young girl, he felt like running back to the hills.

He looked up and found the lass regarding him with her bonny blue eyes.

'What's your name?'

'Hamish.'

'Mine is Maggie. If you promise you will come and bide at my mother's hoose for the month, then I will let you go. We can teach you a little about true strength.'

'Anything!' wailed Hamish, 'just please let me go! You're hurtin me!'

Maggie released her grip and tutted with dismay when she saw how swollen Hamish's huge hand had become. 'Come awa' then, doon to the hoose. We'll soon have you sorted!'

When the two reached the farm, a woman appeared from the barn. Around her neck, she had a cow.

'Mornin' Maggie! I'm jist awa' wi' Daisy up the hill! And who's this?'

'Mother, this is Hamish. He's come for a wee bit o' tutorin' fae us. He's goin' tae the Tarland show!'

'Ah! Welcome, Hamish! I'll be back in a wee while!'

Hamish nodded and gulped. He felt like his whole world had been turned upside down.

'Hamish, there's Gran. She's jist woken up.'

The young man turned to see a doddery old woman stepping out of the farmhouse door. Instead of walking around the cherry tree that was leaning across her path, she tripped over one of the roots and fell flat on her face. Before Maggie or Hamish could run up the path to help her, the old granny sprung up like a young thing, grasped the tree by its trunk and hauled it out of the ground as if it were a weed, throwing it so it flew and landed on the grass. Muttering to herself, she wiped her hands, then looked up and saw Maggie. Her face broke into a toothless smile. 'Maggie! Mornin'! I've finally hed enough o' that geen tree! Can ye get it awa' lass?'

'Aye Gran, nae bother!' Maggie picked her way through flowerbeds to where the fallen tree lay, and effortlessly clasped it around the trunk, tossing it up and over her shoulder. The tree rose into the air, higher and higher, and as Hamish watched, it began its descent, landing about halfway up the hill from where he had come.

Maggie wrinkled her nose. 'Hmmm, I'll shift it over the brow later, but for now, Granny, this is …' She turned to introduce Hamish, but it had all been a bit much and he had fainted.

When he came to, Gran was peering down at him with concern. 'Are you aright, laddie?'

Hamish sat up and looked around. He was in the neat little farmhouse, lying on a couch. Suddenly the morning's events came rushing back, and with them pangs of hunger. His belly began to complain, and Granny smiled.

'Sounds like you need some food, Hamish!' She bustled over to the fire and from a huge pot ladled out some very thick porridge.

'Noo ma lad, get that doon ye! And efter that, Maggie has asked me tae start yer lessons!'

The porridge was so lumpy that Hamish had to chew each bite for a very long time to swallow, and his jaws were aching by the end of the meal. And that was just the beginning. Gran began to wrestle with Hamish, but every time, he landed on his back; she was slippery as an eel, and her strength! By the time the afternoon light was fading, Hamish had a very healthy respect for the old woman.

The short days fell into a regular pattern which saw Hamish up before dawn to exercise and run with Maggie, who strode ahead within minutes of them setting off. There were three meals a day, and with each one, Hamish had less and less water added to his porridge, and with constant masticating, his jaws were becoming like steel.

Most days were spent with Gran, who put him through his paces and seemed never to rest despite her frail appearance. The weeks passed, and on the third-to-last day before his departure, Hamish finally managed to make Gran bend her knee. What joy there was in the household that night, and more celebration when

the next day, Hamish uprooted and tossed a rowan tree as easily as if it were a thistle!

On his final night at the farm, Maggie's mother said, 'Hamish, ye've been such a good pupil. Ye've never complained, and I believe ye've gained a lot o' wisdom frae my mother.'

Hamish looked round at the three smiling faces glowing in the firelight, and his heart was full.

'Thank ye so much for a ye've done for me, especially you Gran. I am so grateful tae ye for takin' me in and showing me jist what true strength is about.' The young man turned to Maggie.

'Maggie, I dinna ken if I am worthy o' ye, but I would like to ask fer ye to marry me and keep me from gettin above masel!'

Maggie's face flushed with pleasure and her blue eyes sparkled. 'Weel awa' an win the competition, and if you still want to come back efter, I'll be waitin!'

With great ceremony, all four climbed the steep path to where Hamish had to journey on, and Gran even permitted him to carry her.

'Noo laddie, dinna forget. Use yer strength, and nae a braggin moo!'

Hamish lowered the old woman gently to the ground and gave each of the women a gallant kiss, although his mouth lingered longer on Maggie's cheek.

When Hamish at last reached Tarland, it was already very busy with competitors, buyers, sellers, young and old all coming for fun and excitement. But the young man did not seek out the inn, but rather he chose to drink some water from the well and eat a slice of the porridge that Maggie had made for him before he left.

The following morning, the day dawned bright and clear. Hamish stretched in his sleeping place behind a shed and unwrapped his plaid. Before the events began, he ran 15 miles and hauled up three trees on a far hill, managing to throw them a fair distance.

He recognised many of the other men who were competing, and smiled warmly at them. This took most of them by surprise, as they had expected Hamish MacInnes to be his usual bragging self. They watched him suspiciously, wondering at the change.

Tossing the caber was the first sport in which Hamish was to compete. He was third in line, and the second man, Jock Pirie, had thrown his caber further than any other man had ever managed before!

Hamish entered the ring and glanced back at Jock, who was looking smug. He nodded his head politely, then with one hand lifted the caber as if it were a feather, and with a flick of his wrist, it flew into the air until it was just a speck. Every eye goggled as it landed away in the woods on the far side of the road. With a wail, Jock Pirie ran from the field, and was found later drowning his sorrows at the inn.

Hamish decided he would not enter every event, as that would be unfair, but the wrestling saw him able to stand as solid as an oak despite some of the competitors being far larger than he. As the day wore on, Hamish saw how many of the strong men were carrying far too much extra weight, some of which was from the excesses of food and drink. Hamish, on the other hand, was lean and mighty muscle, all thanks to the three strong women who had trained him for the last month.

The final event was the running race; the winner would be the first man to make it up the hill and back. Although Hamish knew he could still not race against Maggie and win, he was humbled to find that he was very much the fastest and most resilient runner on the hill that day.

Hamish was saddened to find that his wonderful successes brought him no popularity, although folk remarked on his lack of strutting pride. In the crowd, he found himself standing alone as the judges tallied up the final results. But the cheering was genuine as he went up to receive first overall prize for the men. As he shook one of the judge's hands, the man stared at him. 'Hamish MacInnes?'

'That's me.'

'I hiv a favour tae ask o' ye!'

'Aye?'

'Wid ye be sae kind as tae nae enter these games again, fur I dinna think anyone will want tae compete against you again!'

Hamish smiled. 'I dinna intend tae compete again, sir. I'm affa happy I've won, and the prize money is affa good, so dinna worry, I winna be back!'

The judge smiled, relieved at that, and clapped Hamish on the back in a friendly manner.

As for Hamish, he was glad to leave Tarland that day and return to the wee glen. There he found the three women, and as far as I know, he married Maggie, and they lived happily together for the rest of their lives. But if ever you hear a thumping from the hills, it may be that Maggie and Hamish are having a toss the tree competition.

Mary Elphinstone

Mary Elphinstone's story is well known in this area, and her grave can still be found within the graveyard at Inverurie in front of the Bass, the remains of a motte and bailey castle from the eleventh century. – G.B.

Reverend Elphinstone and his wife were well known and well-loved faces in the village; Mary wheeling along her pram with the latest child, while the other two were swung down the road clutching their father's hands. Everyone agreed they were a delightful family, and that the parish was fortunate to have them. But one year, Mary's health began to fail, and each sickness seemed to lead to another, leaving the lithe, bonny woman frail and thin. For a while, it appeared she was beginning to rally, but one cold autumn day, she suddenly had to take to her bed. To the distress of all those who loved her, she quickly faltered, her breathing shallow, her skin white as paper as she lost consciousness.

The reverend sat by his wife's side day and night while his spinster sister, Betty, looked after the household and the three children. As time passed, he became more and more haggard, and the kirk folk hardly recognised the hollow-eyed man for the good-natured minister they knew and loved.

It was during the night that Mary Elphinstone quietly slipped away. Her husband had fallen into a dead sleep in a chair at her side, and he was only woken by the maid coming in to light the

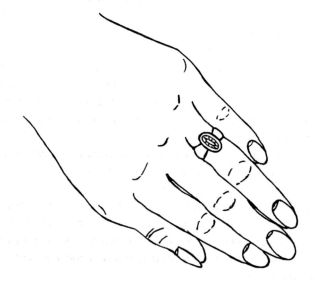

fire. Imagine the reverend's grief to find Mary cold and still, her life's breath gone from her wasted frame, yet her glorious red hair still as vivid as when he first met her.

'Betty, I canna bear tae let ma Mary go.'

Betty looked up from her mending. It was the day before the funeral, and she had been fitting out her brother's suit. She was bone tired, trying to care for all four of the family, as well as from coping with her own grief, for Mary had been like the sister Betty never had. 'Dod, it's hard on us a', but you havna' got a choice. Has the coffin been sealed yet?'

Dod sat down carelessly, resting his head on the back of the chair, and closed his eyes. 'I jist took the bairns in tae say a last goodbye ... they a' hed a word wi' her, an noo they're a sleepin'. I'm jist awa' back in.'

Betty nodded silently. There was nothing more to be said.

'She looks like she's sleepin.'

Betty looked up once more. 'Aye, she's affa bonny in her weddin' goon an her ring. Are ye keepin the ring for yer bairns?' Dod shook his head firmly. 'No, it belongs tae Mary. She's takin it wi' her.'

Betty smiled gently at her brother. 'Aye, Dod. Noo I hiv tae finish yer jaiket.'

Dod stood up shakily. He had not been eating, and he felt sick. 'Right, I'll awa' through.'

The following day, the kirk was crowded, and a neighbouring minister took the proceedings while Dod clung to his bewildered children. Only Betty managed to be at the graveside, while her brother took the little ones back to the house to grieve in the privacy of their very empty home.

The wake took place at the local inn, and food had been provided by many of the parish women. This attracted both those who knew the Elphinstones, and many who did not. Sat in one corner of the inn was Sandy. He was passing through, and just happened to fall lucky onto this free evening meal. He was enjoying the craic and the ale when he overhead two women talking close by. The fiddles were tuning up, so they raised their voices and Sandy heard every word.

'Ye ken, she wis so bonny in her weddin dress. The reverend let a' the maids hae time wi' her tae say oor goodbyes.'

'He's sich a kind man, an' it's sich a shame!'

'Aye, but Peggy, he lo'ed her so much he's buried her wi' her ring on!'

'Oh?'

'Aye! An the ring has a big ruby in it!'

'No?'

'Aye!' said the maid, nodding emphatically, 'it's HUGE!'

'Fit a waste!'

At that moment, fiddle music blared out, obliterating any conversation. Sandy smiled to himself. Freshly buried and not far away? He'd passed the graveyard earlier on his way into town, and had seen the sombre crowd milling out of the gates in the pouring rain. The grave should be easy to find … he was used to such work.

The wake was still in full spate when Sandy quietly left. It was a cold, dark night, but now dry; perfect for the kind of work he was about to do. He found the road back to the graveyard and silently walked towards the gates. He stopped, listening. He did not know if there were any guards on duty, to watch for grave robbers. But there was only silence, and carefully he grasped the handle and swung the gate outward. It let out a violent squeak that made him jump and set his heart racing. Again he stopped, waiting for the hammering in his chest to subside, but there was no pelt of running footsteps, just the sound of his own ragged breathing.

Sandy had no idea in which part of the cemetery the woman had been buried. He would have to light a match and look for the tell-tale signs of tracked mud. He bent low to the ground, struck the match, shading the flare, and scanned in front of him. Sure enough, off to the left, there was a trail of muddy footprints. He let the match die and walked in the direction of the prints.

Although he had been in many graveyards in his time, Sandy nevertheless felt extremely uncomfortable. The darkness and the silence pressed down on him oppressively as the ground began to rise under his feet. It was impossible to see anything, and Sandy's imagination had all kinds of creatures stealthily creeping in his direction. Despite the cold, sweat began to bead on his forehead, and his breath came in gasps. A sudden scream overhead scared him so badly he almost toppled over, but the sound of wings passing close by made him almost swoon in relief. It was an owl.

In the blinding dark, it took Sandy a long time to find the grave of Mary Elphinstone. But once there, he settled into the task. From the sack flung over his shoulder, he took out a folding spade and began to dig. It was hot work, and soon his jacket was off. Although the dark hampered his sense of direction, it was not long before he heard the clunk of metal on wood. Using his hands and spade, he cleared the top of the coffin, then, taking a candle from his trouser pocket, he lit it and dug it into the mud, where it gave out a small light for him to see and begin the next phase. Taking out a variety of screwdrivers from beneath his coat, Sandy found one that matched the brass screws on the lid of the coffin, and deftly loosened them off.

Straddling the grave, he carefully lifted off the lid and laid it to one side. Taking his candle, he knelt down at the side of the coffin to view his prize. Sandy was very aware of the dead woman that lay before him. Her wedding dress glowed so white in the candlelight. He felt very uncomfortable, but he averted his eyes from her face, and instead scanned her hands. Sure enough, it was as the maid had said, there was the magnificent ring!

'Worth a' the trouble,' the robber muttered quietly, a gleeful grin on his face. He placed the candle on the ground, and in one hand he raised up the corpse's cold and clammy palm, and with his other hand, he began to pull at the ring on her finger. It was stuck, so he tried once more, tugging a bit harder. The flickering of the candle cast strange shadows over the figure in the coffin, and Sandy could feel his hands sweating as he twisted and turned the ring every which way and howked at it in a very uncivilised manner. He was beginning to panic now. He felt the whole host of the graveyard was watching his wicked deed, and would rise up against him at any moment.

In desperation, Sandy took out his penknife and flicked it open. Bending once more over the shrouded figure, he took hold of the ring finger, and set about it, hacking and sawing. Blood began to spurt out from beneath the blade, and suddenly there was a bloodcurdling scream from the very mouth of the dead woman. Terrified, Sandy fell backwards, his own screeching mingling with that of the banshee in the coffin. Weeping and mumbling, the hysterical man stumbled out of the graveyard and left Inverurie forever.

It was the dead of night when Dod was woken by the sound. He could hear knocking at the front door. Bleary-eyed and confused, he lit a candle, and wrapping himself in a blanket, made his way downstairs towards the frantic rapping.

'Dod! Dod!' came a muffled call. The minister froze. There was no mistaking it. That voice was familiar, and belonged to only one person.

'Mary?' he cried, his hands shaking. What was this? A cruel dream, a ghost come to haunt him? His heart was beating loudly, but he was drawn to the voice, and found himself turning the key in the lock and pulling the door open. With a trembling hand, he lifted the candle high to squint out into the dark. There before him, ghastly in white, streaked with vermillion-red blood, was his dead Mary.

But Mary was very much alive. The doctor had mistaken a deep coma for death. Her peripheries had become cold, and there was hardly a pulse – it was nigh imperceptible. The shock of having her finger half-sawn off had been enough to pull the woman out of her unconscious state. She had managed to climb out of her grave, stumble her way through the pitch-black graveyard, and home to the manse.

At first terrifying her husband, Mary was joyfully brought back into the love of her family. The couple had many more years together, before Dod and Mary died within a few years of each other.

2

THE LAND

THE TATTIEBOGLE

The first time that Stanley Robertson told me this story, it was eerie, dark, with no love interest at all, and this is the version I've chosen to set down. He gave no setting for it, but it sits well in the Howe o' Cromar, so there I have placed it. I have another reason for doing this. The incantation that Stanley used to make the scarecrow come alive is the following:

'A laird, a lord, a lily, a leaf, a piper, a drummer, a hummer, a thief.'

My grandmother, Lizzie Philip of Coull, regularly recited that rhyme to me as a toddler, and it was also used as we placed prune stones round our dish of custard …

The Howe of Cromar suffered from crows attacking its crops and from MacGregors stealing its cattle. A cave at the Burn o' Vat, on the Muir of Dinnet, was their hideout, known locally (and erroneously) as Rob Roy's Cave. It was, in fact, Gilderoy MacGregor's lair, and I've added Gilderoy's ballad to conclude the tale. – S.B.

In medieval times, farmers believed that the scarecrows they made had special powers. In the North-East of Scotland, they are called tattiebogles, but in other places in Europe they are bootzamonor, shoy-hoy, or Jack-in-the-straw. Italians set the skulls of animals on high poles in the fields, whereas Germans made wooden witches, driving them into their lands at the end of winter. They thought that the evil spirit of winter crept into those witches, allowing spring to arrive. Before the plague, when people were many, young boys or girls patrolled the fields, scaring off the birds. After the death of so many in that great scourge, farmers stuffed sacks with straw, and carved faces in turnips set upon sticks.

Cromar, or *Crò Mhàrr* in the old Gaelic tongue, is the most fertile valley of Deeside, encircled by a sweep of hills dominated by Morven, with Lochnagar in the distance. Its principal villages are Tarland and Logie Coldstone near to the Muir of Dinnet. Folk have lived here since 4000 BC, and have left behind their markers; the eerie stone circle at Tomnaverie, a souterrain at Culsh and many burial cairns, lesser stone circles, Bronze Age fortifications and Pictish stones. On the shoulder of Morven is Culblean, which the Burn o' Vat runs through. The burn carved a cauldron-like gorge in the pink granite, the hideout of the infamous seventeenth-century outlaw Gilderoy MacGregor.

After the civil war, Highlanders roamed freely about Cromar looting, plundering and cattle-stealing. Local farmers joined together to hire a band of MacGregors from Perthshire, headed by Gilderoy, as mercenaries to protect their cows. Gilderoy's band turned rustlers themselves, hiding in the gorge at the Burn o' Vat, and driving cattle off over the high heathery drove roads at will.

This proclamation was issued by the Privy Council in March 1636:

Patrick MacGregor (aka Gilderoy) and others hes associat and combynned themselves togidder, hes thair residence neere to the forests of Culblene (Culblean) … and from these parts they come in darknes of the night down to the incountrie, falls unaware upon the houses and goods of his Majesties poore subjects and spoyles theme of their goods, and, being full handed with the spoyle they goe backe agane to the bounds forsaids where they keepe mercat of thair goods peaceablie and uncontrolled, to the disgrace of law and order. For the remeid whairof the Lords of Secreit Counsell charge all landslord and heretours, where thir brokin lymmars has thair resset, abode, and starting holes, to rise, putt thamselffes in arnes, and to hunt, follow and persew, shout and raise the fray, and with fire and sword to persew the saids theeves, and never leave aff thair persute till they be ather apprehended or putt out of the countrye.

Put clearly – Wanted: Dead or Alive!

When one farmer, Akey Broon, went to the wedding of his friend John Tam, he came back to find the heather thatch of his house in flames and his cattle gone.

Culblean wis brunt, Cromar wis herriet
Oh, dowie's the day John Tam wis merriet!

With much trouble and sorrow, he managed to rebuild his little home, but no longer felt inclined to herd cattle. Thinking that the MacGregors would not be able to steal and drive off crops, he planted oats and barley, and they would have grown well, for Cromar is fertile, had it not been for the crows which infested the place at that time, worse than any Highland caterans.

The trees seemed to grow crows like black fruit, ready to fly down and strip a newly-sown field bare as a bone. After a great deal of thought and worry, he decided to visit the Warlock Stane at Craiglash where, 100 years before, the great warlock Colin Massie had met with his coven of witches. He went by back roads around midnight to the mighty stone near to Potarch. It was raining, and queer lights seemed to be moving through the trees. The coven was put to the torch during the Aberdeen Witch Trials of 1596–97, but so great was the power of the witches that local folk believed their ghosts still inhabited the area.

There was Margret Clarke of Lumphanan, found guilty of killing John Burnett. As he rode by on horseback, she 'lurkit back towards him and cast up her hands and mumbled some of her devilish prayers'. Soon after, he took to his bed and died. There was Janet Davidson of Sundayswells, who killed Patrick Hunter with her 'diverse writings of witchcraft'. There was Helen Rogie of Findtrack; her speciality was making 'pictours' of her victims (a pictour is an image of soft lead or wax). At her trial, she was accused of having 'roasted sundry times the pictours of men whome [thou] murdered'. There was Margret Ogg, who bewitched her neighbour's cattle. There was Janet Lucas, found with a magical charm of coloured thread in her purse when arrested at the kirk in Lumphanan. There was Isobel Ogg of Craigtown of Lumphanan who used witchcraft to aid two Banchory women in outselling their rivals at the market. And finally, there was their lord and master, Colin Massie of Glendye, the warlock who, like his ancient mother, could take the form of a futterat or hare. His mother cheated the stake by being shot by young Russel of Tillyfroskie, who loaded his gun with a silver sixpence.

All had been imprisoned in the Tolbooth in Aberdeen, and tortured with thumbscrews, red-hot leg irons, heavy weights, the witch bridle and the ducking stool. They brought in much money to Aberdeen's hangman, John Justice. He was paid 13/4d an execution. Each witch was bound to a stake and verreit (strangled) before being burned. But standing at midnight by the Warlock Stane, Akey Broon knew perfectly well that their dark spirits were still abroad.

It was the warlock himself, Colin Massie, who showed himself finally, by voice only, deep, but steady and clear. He passed on a spell given to him by the Devil himself for creating the most powerful of all tattiebogles.

First, you must pull a turnip from the field, and gouge out sockets for its eyes and mouth. You must cut the yellow eyes from a barn owl, stoned to death, and cut the mouth from a child dead of the smallpox. Place those in the turnip, and they will take root.

Now dig out an eye from seven corpses; a rabbit, a cow, a deer, a snake, a salmon, a badger, a wildcat, and sew them on as buttons for the jacket. Press the turnip onto a pole and add on the jacket, trouser and boots, all stuffed with straw. Then you must cut a pair of hands from a corpse on the gibbet, and pull out its rotten heart to place inside the coat. Be careful nobody's near to see or hear you. To make it come alive, repeat the words of this magic spell: A laird, a lord, a lily, a leaf, a piper, a drummer, a hummer, a thief.

Once Akey Broon had gathered the gruesome bits and pieces together, he did as the warlock had told him. Instantly, the yellow eyes of the tattiebogle blinked alive, and the terrified crows flew off far into the woodlands, screeching. The head, like that of an owl, swivelled on its stick. It was the most evil looking of things between Heaven and Hell.

All that year, Akey Broon's crops grew well, while the crows ravaged the fields of his neighbours. Next year, blight killed the crops, over which the tattiebogle had no power, and yet it was powerful for all that, and if anything its power was growing. Akey started drinking heavily, and one day in despair, he walked into the middle of the field with a scythe and sliced off the tattiebogle's dead hand. The creature screamed, and the hand wriggled around on the earth. Scared, Akey ran back towards the farm, but tripped and fell on his own scythe blade, cutting his left hand off.

Now, it was almost impossible for Akey to scratch a living, crippled as he was. He lay in bed one night, tossing and turning, and seeking revenge in his fuddled mind for this injury he was sure

was caused by the tattiebogle. He lifted his scythe again and left the house. This time, he crept up behind it in the dark, raised the scythe and beheaded it, just as the turnip head with the yellow eyes whirled round to stare up at him. The next day, he was found near the Muir of Dinnet, babbling insanely. He was trussed up and taken away to bedlam, where he died soon after.

The next man to take on the farm knew nothing of this. He was a cattleman, who preferred raising herds to corn, and luckily for him, he arrived as Gilderoy MacGregor and his band were finally caught and taken down to Edinburgh, where in 1658, they were hanged.

Riddle Three
Softly I come, quiet in the snow
Yet brightly I beckon others to grow
All is awakening, hope I bring
Look to me to tell you of Spring.

THE BALLAD OF GILDEROY

My love he was as brave a man as ever Scotland bred.
Descended from a Highland Clan, a cateran to his trade
No woman then or woman now had ever greater joy
Than we two when we lodg'd alone, I and my Gilderoy.

First when I and my Love met, with Joy he did me crown,
He gave me a new Petticoat, and then a Tartan Gown:
Gilderoy was a bonny Boy when he went to the Glen,
He had silk Stockens, on his Legs, and Roses in his Shoon

When Gilderoy went to the wood, he oft-times catch'd the Fat,
Into the Desert as he went, scarce ten durst bell the cat
But if he were as stout as Wallace, tall as Dalmahoy,
He'd never miss to get a clout from my love Gilderoy.

When Gilderoy and I was young, we was brought up together,
And we were scarce seven years old, when the one did love the other;
Our Fathers and our Mothers both, they thought of us great joy,
And long'd to see the Wedding-day 'twixt me and Gilderoy.

Till it fell once upon a time they catch'd him like a thief,
And ty'd his Hands behind his back, which was to me great grief;
Three Gallons large of Usquebaugh, they drank to my Love's Foy,
And in to Edinburgh they have ta'en my gallant Gilderoy.

A pox upon your English Laws, that hangs a Man for Gear,
Either for catching cow or ewe, or stealing horse or mare;
Had not their Laws been made so strict, I'd never lost my Joy;
But now he's gone whom I love best, I mean my Gilderoy.

And now he is in Edinburgh Town, 'twas long e're I came there,
They hangèd him upon a Pin, and he wagged in the Air:
His relicks they were more esteem'd, than Scanderbeg or Troy;
And that was how they dealt with him, my darling Gilderoy.

The Highwayman and the Orra Loon

I have heard and read many tales about life in the North-East of Scotland and this one has remained with me and become a firm favourite. – G.B.

Some distance west of Huntly, Blackhill the farmer was in quite a predicament. It had been a prosperous summer, and the harvest had been safely brought in. The time of year was approaching where farm workers would have completed their six months' feeing and were due payment, but Blackhill had no money to give his hands. He dared not travel to the bank in Huntly, for on the road to town lurked a highwayman. This robber was wily enough never to have been caught, and many travellers had fallen victim to

him, suffering theft and injury at his hands.

There was a chill in the air as Blackhill came out from the stables. Already the long summer days were giving way to the darkened skies of autumn. Blackhill sighed. He had tried to persuade some of his workers to go in his place to Huntly to collect the wages, but even when offered a large bonus, each one had refused. The farmer could not blame them for their decision.

Blackhill began to trudge back towards the farmhouse where his wife Betty would have his fly-cup waiting. But then, coming from the field, he saw a slight figure running towards him. 'Sir! Sir!' It was the youngest employee at the farm, the orra loon, Donald.

'Aye, Donald. What is it?'

The boy stopped in front of his master, breathless, and trying to find his words. 'I'll ... awa' ... tae Huntly ... fer ye!' Blackhill looked down at the grubby face looking up at him earnestly, his thatch of hair gleaming gold in the last rays of the sun. The farmer scratched his bristly chin. 'Donald, ye ken there's a robber on the road?'

'Aye, I ken, but that disnae bother me, maister,' he said, smiling.

Blackhill frowned. He had no one else to turn to, but would this young lad, not the brightest penny, actually manage to return with the wages? It was a great risk. Eventually, Blackhill said, 'Weel, lad, that's verra kind o' ye tae offer. Ye'll gang the morn, and ye maun tak Bess, ma fastest horse. An ye mustn't stop fir anybody on the road.'

'Aye, maister ... I ken ... aye ... no ... I winna ...'

'Tak the big saddlebags fir a' the wages.'

The lad nodded, his face beaming. 'Dinna fash, maister, I'll bring them back!'

The next morning, Blackhill hurried down at first light to ensure that Donald was prepared, but discovered with dismay that the lad was already gone, not on Bess, but Archie, the old white nag, who was fit for nothing but eating choice bits of hay. The farmer groaned, and asked the stablehand, 'Fit time wis he awa', Bill?'

'He rose hoors ago, maister. He'll be well on the wye noo.'

And Donald was! He was well over halfway to Huntly, and it was a fine morning to be trudging over hill and through glen, even at Archie's slow trot. Flashes of burnished yellow and orange were beginning to touch the leaves on the trees, and a mild breeze was blowing in Donald's face as he gnawed on a hunk of bread from his pocket. The road had been winding upwards, and the view beyond the rise made the lad smile in pleasure. He gently nudged the old horse. 'Come on, Archie, it's doon the wye noo!'

Ahead, the road wandered by a thick forest of pines. As the lad and horse approached, a dark mounted figure emerged from beneath the trees and stood still in the middle of the road.

Donald seemed not in the least perturbed. 'Mornin'!' he called, waving a hand cheerily at the stranger. He could see pistols at the man's waist, winking in the sunlight.

'An whaur are ye awa' tae the day, lad?'

'I'm awa' tae get Blackhill's money fae the bank tae pay a' the ferm workers their wages!'

The man's eyes seemed to pierce Donald through, then a breath of a smile touched his lips. 'Weel, I'll mebbe travel the road wi' ye lad fer a while. Fit's yer name?'

'I'm Donald, sir, an I'd be gled o' company!'

For the next mile or two, this incongruous pair trotted along, the slight lad on his old white nag and the sturdy, well-dressed man on his glossy black steed. Donald could talk for Scotland, and hardly ceased until the man turned and said, 'Right Donald, I'll awa' noo. It's been guid tae meet ye, an I'll mebbe see ye again.'

'Aye, thank ye, sir! Cheerio!'

Donald reached Huntly without further incident, and followed his master's instructions closely, except in one thing – he had taken along two sets of saddlebags. In one, he stored the wages, and in the other, he put stones. He tied both up very strongly, and fixed them onto Archie's saddle. After enjoying some refreshment, Donald mounted up once more for Blackhill.

As Donald approached the pine forest, the afternoon sun was casting dark shapes on the road ahead. He could see a familiar figure waiting in the shadows. The highwayman hailed Donald as he came closer. 'Donald!'

'Hello, sir!'

'Noo, lad, tak yer saddlebags an throw them doon on the road!'

Donald's face was frozen in distress. 'But sir! I hiv tae tak the money back tae ma maister!' The robber drew out his pistols. 'Donald, dee as I say, noo!'

The lad looked terrified, and said in panic, 'Aye! I will, dinna shoot!' He fumbled with the saddlebags, and clumsily flung them as far as his thin arms possibly could. They landed in a ditch on the far side of a fence that lined the forest.

Cursing angrily, the robber dismounted and stalked over to the fence. He was forced to crouch down to get under overhanging branches, and then climb over the fence. While his back was turned to Donald, the lad clambered down from Archie with the other saddlebags over his shoulder. He quickly grabbed the reins of the robber's beautiful black horse and hauled himself up into the saddle. With a sharp dig from Donald's heels and a tug at the reins, the horse turned, and away they galloped, the lad bent low over the animal's neck.

At the sound of hooves, the highwayman looked back to see his horse disappearing up the brae. With a roar of rage, the red-faced man struggled over the fence, fumbling to reach for his pistol while trying to shove branches out of his way with the heavy saddlebags in one hand. 'Ye wee trickster!' he shouted furiously, for Donald had escaped.

Blackhill was relieved and a little confused when he saw Donald galloping into the farm on a very different steed from the one he had left on. There was great celebration at the farm that night. The orra loon was regarded a hero, and was well rewarded by a very grateful farmer. His story gave much amusement to all who heard it, and gained Donald much respect. But there was not much joy in it for a certain highwayman, who had ended up with a bag of stones and no horse because of a deceptively simple-looking young man.

About ten years later, Donald happened to be enjoying a mug of ale at an inn when he heard two men enter. The room had partitions between each table for privacy, but the men placed themselves adjacent to where Donald was sitting, and he could not but help hear their conversation, especially as one man's voice was raised so loudly.

'Aye, that skinny wee trickster left me wi' a saddlebag fu' o' stones an' nae horse!' Donald's eyes widened, suddenly very aware of the danger he was in, but he listened all the more carefully.

The man's companion murmured sympathetically, but the former highwayman was not finished. 'An that's nae a'! He didna' ken it, but stitched intae ma saddlebag wis a the money I hid stolen frae fowk o'er the last year! An' it wis a lost tae that wee runt!'

Donald's pint had been halfway to his mouth, but his hand stopped in mid-air, and he grinned an ear-splitting smile before raising the tankard to his lips.

The following week, Donald made time to travel back to Blackhill where he had spent his first year as a farm worker. It had been another good year, and as he looked over the farm with a keener eye, he saw it was in fine shape. He found Blackhill working in the byre. 'Mr Blackhill!'

The farmer turned, and saw the tall young man standing in the doorway. He screwed up his eyes. 'Donald? Is that you, loon?'

'Aye, sir, it's me. I thocht ye'd ken me!'

'Aye, I nivver forget a face, ye ken, though ye've grown!' exclaimed Blackhill, smiling. 'Fit are ye doin here lad?'

When Donald explained his reason for visiting, the farmer's eyes grew wide. 'Come awa' then, Donald! I dinna ken if we still hae that saddle!'

It took a good long time to find, but eventually they unearthed it. The leather was cracked and had darkened with age. 'Go on lad, you dee it!' said Blackhill, handing Donald a knife. Donald took the saddle and cut deep across a seam. It sprang back, revealing a great wealth and variety of notes and coins!

Needless to say, Blackhill was very generous to this honest and resourceful young man. With his reward, Donald was able to start his own business, which he ran very successfully, continuing to be a wise man in all his dealings.

An Aul Beggarman

When I first began to hear and learn the songs of the North-East I heard Kathleen Stewart singing this song. It tells the story of a beggar man who is not who he appears to be! The pictures are very vivid and I found I liked the tune. It was one I learned quickly, and now it is like an old friend to greet and enjoy from time to time. – G.B.

An aul beggarman cam o'er yon lea
Seekin alms for charity
Seekin alms for charity
'Wid y lodge an aul beggarman?'
Liddle lilty tow row rae.

The nicht wis caul an the carle wis weet
As doon by the ingle neuk he sat
He's taen his meal pyocks aff his back
And aye he's ranted and he sang
Liddle lilty tow row rae.

Gin I were black as ye are fite
As lang fell snaw ahint yon dyke
I'd dress masel fu beggar-like
And awa' wi' ye I'd gang!'
Liddle lilty tow row rae.

Oh lassie, o' lassie yer far o'er young
An y hinna got the cant o' the beggin tongue
Y hinna got the cant o' the beggin tongue
An wi' me ye canna gang'
Liddle lilty tow row rae.

But I'd bend ma back an I'd bow ma knee
I'd put a black patch o'er ae ee
An a richt guid beggar wife I'd be
An wi' you I want tae gang!'
Liddle lilty tow row rae.

Atween the twa they hae made up a plot
Tae rise twa hoors afore the lot
Sae gently she his slippit the lock
An awa' o'er the fields they ran
Liddle lilty tow row rae.

Early next mornin' the aul wife arose
An eagerly she's pit on her clothes
Strecht tae the servant she did gang
Sayin, 'Fire for the silly aul man!'
Liddle lilty tow row rae.

The servant she gaed far the beggar lay
But his sheets were caul an he wis awa'
Strecht tae the aul wife she did say,
'Hes ony o' oor guid gear gane?'
Liddle lilty tow row rae.

Some gaed tae the coffer and some tae the kist
But naethin wis stolen nor yet wis missed
An she's lifted up her hans sayin, 'Guid be praised
We hae lodged an honest beggarman!'
Liddle lilty tow row rae.

The servant she gaed far the lassie lay
But her sheets were caul an she wis awa'
Strecht tae the aul wife she did say
'She's awa' wi' the aul beggarman!'
Liddle lilty tow row rae.

Some gaed on horseback an some gaed on fit
Except for the aul wife for she wisna fit
An she's hoppit about fae hip tae hip
And aye she's cursed an she's banned
Liddle lilty tow row rae.

A few years later, mebbe twa or three
An aul beggarman cam o'er yon lea
Sayin, 'Aul wife for yer charity
Wid y lodge an aul beggarman?'
Liddle lilty tow row rae.

A beggar, a beggar I'll ne'er lodge again
For I aince hed a dochter, een o' ma ain
But awa' wi' a beggar she hes gaen
An I dinna ken fence or far
Liddle lilty tow row rae.

'Uh! Aul wifie, aul wifie fit wid ye gie
For a glimpse o' yer dochter aince mair tae see
Wi een at her back, an een at her knee
An een on the road comin hame!'
Liddle lilty tow row rae.

'For yonder she's comin tae yer bower
Wi monys the satins an monys the floor!'
An she's lifted up her hans an she's praised the hoor
That she lodged an aul beggarman
Liddle lilty tow row rae.

The Gudeman o' Ballengeich

James V was a man of the people. It is said that he would put on a disguise and, calling himself the Gudeman of Ballengeich, he would walk amongst his people and share in their hospitality.

On one occasion, the king had been travelling for some days, his beggar's garb insufficient for a Deeside winter of snow-packed ground, ice-cold wind and a damp that had frozen his feet inside his worn shoes. He stumbled on a little cottar house near to Kinker or Kincardine o' Neil and desperately knocked on the door.

Now this was a poor house, and in very bad repair. Two sons this couple had, but both had been taken for soldiers to fight in the king's wars and there was no young blood to thatch the roof, replace timbers or mend the fencing. Cochran did his best, but his cattle were depleted and he had no means to buy more. The little the couple made was just enough to tide them over. The roof was bowed with snow, the wind found its way through many cracks and the wee home never really warmed up, despite the blazing fire that Mrs Cochran made each day.

But when a knock came to their door on that snowy, sleety windy night, Flora, the wife, flung the door wide. Seeing the wet stranger, she ushered him in, clucking over him like a broody hen. She took his sopping cloak and bade him sit close to the fire.

He was in luck, she said, they had just eaten and so the food she had been about to prepare was all to be for him. With that the wee wiry woman disappeared out into that miserable night, dressed in her thin plaid. It was a good while before she returned. She was blue with cold and her hands were white and bleeding. But clutched in them were three miserable-looking frozen turnips.

'Guid neeps! See! Twill mak' a fine broth tae y!' Cochran looked longingly at the food. He had not had a bite to eat all day and was dropping with fatigue, but it was the way of this couple; the stranger aye was given the best of what was in the house.

So the guest found his clothes steaming gently as first the turnips were thawed and howked into pieces, then placed in the black pot over the fire. The king's belly was groaning with hunger; he would have eaten the vegetables raw if he could! After what seemed like an age the wee woman thrust a wooden bowl into his hand and the good smell of the wholesome soup wafted up his nostrils. The guest ate bowlful after bowlful until there were just scrapings left in the pot.

The king was not insensitive to this poor couple's plight. Well, he saw Cochran's hungry eyes follow every spoonful into his mouth, and although he had been starving himself, it had taken much willpower for the king to carry on eating with relish, knowing that Cochran and his wife had gone without food themselves.

The king was well wrapped up in various covers and passed a cosy night in front of the fire, while Cochran and his wife shivered in their box bed, with very little to keep the cold out.

'Weel hiv y slept fine noo?'

'Aye I hiv thank you Mrs Cochran. It wis rare to be so warm!'

Flora beamed with pleasure, 'That's fine! Noo I hiv made some porridge tae y! Come awa' up on the stool!'

'Och Mrs Cochran, I feel like I'm yer son!'

A shadow passed over the wee woman's face. 'Ach, ma bairns ...' she sighed.

'Far are yer bairns?'

Flora's face changed and when she turned her eyes on the king, he started to see this mild, cheery woman so full of anger. 'The king took them awa'! Greedy man! Noo dinna get me wrang! I like the king, but he hes no idea fit a boorach ma man and I are in wioot oor loons!'

Her normally jovial face crumpled. 'It's sich a worry, oor wee bit o' pairks an beasts an this hoose a goin tae rack an' ruin ... for ma man canna look efter it ony langer! The king wid niver hiv tae suffer like this! An he's taken oor bairns awa', loons that could help their Faither and Mither at sich a herd time!'

The king was very distressed. He comforted Mrs Cochran as best he could but he was glad when her husband came in through the door, having just fed the cattle.

Mrs Cochran pulled herself together and busied herself at the fire.

When their guest had been plied full of porridge and could not be persuaded to 'bide another day', the couple bid him farewell and offered him their hospitality if ever he was to come that way again.

'Many thanks Mr and Mrs Cochran, you hiv baith been maist kind an I winna forget yer generosity!' He shook their hands solemnly and disappeared down the road into fresh falling snow.

A month later, the Cochrans were just preparing for bed when there was a rattle at the door and in came a big man dressed in a coat and hat. Terrified, the old couple clung together in fear.

'Faither, Mither, d'you nae recognise yer own loon?'

Astonished the couple peered at the man, then Flora let out a screech and hurtled over. 'David!' she cried, trying to hug her son with her thin arms. He reached down and lifted her up in his embrace, 'I'm hame Mither! Hame for guid! The king released me! An' ma brither tae! He'll be hame in a few days!'

Such rejoicing was in that little household that night. And there was more to come.

It was later in the spring, when the trees were all covered in a mist of green that Cochran was distracted from his work by the sound of lowing cattle. He looked up in surprise, thinking his own had somehow escaped the new fence that his other son Peter had raised. But no; along the road, driven by two men on horseback, was a herd of fine looking cows. They stopped outside the fence.

'Mr Cochran?'

'Aye?'

'The king hes asked far wid you like yer new herd o' coos?'

King James returned to Kinker on a beautiful summer's day, not as a beggar but dressed simply as the kind king he was. When he saw the Cochran's house with its newly thatched roof and smelt the good smell of newly-sawn timbers, he smiled with joy and satisfaction.

At his knock Mrs Cochran came hurrying to the door, and he laughed outright when he saw the shock on her face. Mrs Cochran, on seeing the king and realising who he was, felt so ashamed at the poor fare she had offered him that previous winter and regretted the rude words she had spoken to him.

King James took her bird-like hands in one of his, and with the other he raised her face so that her eyes were looking into his.

'Mrs Cochran, never hiv I been fed sich rich food and niver hiv I slept on a safter, warmer bed and niver hiv I hed a truer word spoken tae me by onybody but in your hame! So my thanks tae you.'

Relief and joy flooded into the wee woman's face and a glint came into her eye, 'Weel yer Majesty, I hiv jist been bakin and I wid be verra pleased if you wid partake o' some bannocks wi' ma family and me?'

'I wid be delighted, Mrs Cochran!'

TEMPLAR THUNDER HOLE

Stanley Robertson told me two stories about Deeside knights. The first was called 'The Chivalry' and he claimed it happened in the woods of Pitfodels, which was owned from the sixteenth to the nineteenth century by the Menzies family. In that legend, knights practised 'chivalry' by saving girls who had been seized and hidden, a gallant form of hide and seek on horseback. An elderly knight was in charge of hiding the maiden, and he lowered her deep down into the roots of a hollow, rotten tree. Unfortunately, she was never rescued, as the knight died of a stroke before he could tell the seekers where she was hidden. On wintry nights, her terrified wails are still heard ringing out in the moonlight ... Here now, is the second tale, of which Stanley had several versions. – S.B.

The Order of the Knights of the Temple were long linked to the parish of Maryculter by the Dee. The Templars began as a group of knights who vowed to protect pilgrims en route to Jerusalem. Their earliest home in the Middle East was a wing of the royal palace, which was built on the site of the Temple of Solomon. The Knights Templar were gifted Maryculter by King William the Lion in 1187.

The Templars were both military and religious, and exclusively male. They wore a white robe with a red Maltese cross on the breast. Each knight was allowed to keep three horses and a page, and they normally attended daily services unless on active duty. Two meals were allowed daily, but to these could be added a light snack towards sunset. Brethren ate in twos to ensure that the other did not practise undue austerity. At every meal, wine was served, and then the rule of silence held good, so that prayers might be heard. Multi-coloured clothes were forbidden; black or dusky-brown robes were to be worn by all except the knights. Their clothes were woollen, but from Easter to All Souls a linen shirt might be worn instead.

Their hair was cropped short, but a rough beard was permitted. The secular pursuits of hunting and hawking were forbidden, all but a lion, which they were allowed to kill. Letters were to be opened only in the master's presence. The Templars were to sleep in single beds in their shirts and breeches, with a light kept burning in the dormitory. Most importantly, the Templars were banned from kissing any woman, even their closest kin, strictly obeying their vows of chastity.

The preceptory at Maryculter was founded between 1221 and 1236 by Walter Bisset, Lord of Aboyne. The knights built their own chapel in the grounds, dedicated to St Mary. This chapel became the parish church for Maryculter in 1288. Their star waned, however, and in 1312, the Templar Order was disbanded, their lands and wealth passing to the Knights Hospitallers, including the lands at Maryculter.

This legend concerns Sir Godfrey Wedderburn, a Maryculter Templar Knight, and a beautiful Saracen woman, whom he met during a Crusade in the Holy Land. He had survived the journey to the East, though many of his fellow Crusaders had died of thirst, hunger, sickness or drowning en route. Having arrived, he had marched across the searing hot desert in full armour with very little food and water. He had fought for many months under extreme conditions, harassed by enemies, and at risk of leprosy, fevers, and the rigours of the fierce desert storms.

The Saracen woman was an Eastern princess who saved his life after he was severely wounded fighting in the desert dunes. Her beauty made him forget his vows, and it is said that for a brief time they became lovers. However, when he recovered, little credit to him, Sir Godfrey deserted her and made the long, dangerous journey home to Scotland. Little did he know that the Saracen princess was carrying his child.

Two or three years elapsed. Leaving the infant in the keeping of her handmaidens, the Saracen princess followed her lover back to the preceptory at Maryculter. She arrived in a night of rain and storm. The appearance of a woman at their retreat, and the circumstances surrounding it, caused consternation amongst the Templars. Sir Godfrey was ordered to take his own life. In a split second, he made his choice. Seizing the princess, he lifted her onto the saddle of his horse, and together they rode at full pelt up the hill from the Templars' Church. The other knights were close in pursuit. The lovers had just reached the Crynoch Burn when Sir Godfrey's horse stumbled, pitching the two riders to their deaths. Fatally wounded, the Saracen princess called down an awful curse on the preceptor of the chapel. Her words rose shrill on the wind, a terrible death shriek, and at that, a thunderbolt shot from the sky and killed him. To this day, the preceptor's death site is called the 'Thunderhole', and can be seen on Maryculter Home Farm.

Since that fateful night, men tell of seeing the ghost of a fully armed Templar soldier galloping through the glen and over the hill of Kingcausie, his war cry rising to the moon. And near Corbie Lynne, the spectre of a dusky woman of great beauty is seen sitting mournfully on the rocks, or floating through the dreary woods, singing in a low melodic voice a lament of unspeakable sadness in the Arabic tongue.

Riddle Four
Will you know me when I come?
From loch, sea, to sky
Here am I

The Rat, the Tree and the Dragon

These are three short legends. The first two are from Deeside, the third from near Huntly. – S.B.

The King Rat

There was once a young couple that lived on the hill of Morven, in a house that was overrun by rats. There were fat rats, thin rats, long rats and short rats. There were rats with twitchy whiskers and rats with twitchy tails. They devoured all the bread and oatmeal and even had the audacity to crawl into the couple's bed at night and try to nibble their toes. Not to put it too fine – the rats ruled the roost.

One day the husband set a box trap and managed to catch the King of the Rats. His wife carried the box trap to a nearby hill, Tom Bad nan Speirag. Her husband went with her armed with a heavy hammer, to discuss the situation with their little prisoner.

No sooner was the cage opened than the king rat leapt up under the woman's petticoats. She jumped, she screamed, she twirled like a dervish and ran home shrieking, chased by her husband. Wherever he saw what appeared to be a lump in her clothes, he thumped it with the hammer, assuming it was the rat. As the couple was known for their violent quarrels, the neighbours feared this was an argument that had got out of hand. Everyone thought the husband was trying to kill his wife. Meanwhile, the king rat escaped and was ensconced back in his old home before the pair returned. Never again did the couple try to oust the rats, but a month or so later, they quietly packed up and left.

Coire Craobh an Oir

West of Luibeg, on a slope of Carn Crom, is the corrie named Coire Craobh an Oir, the corrie of the tree of gold. One of the powerful Mackenzies of Dalmore buried his treasure from a raid in Lochaber beside this tree, before moving the gold to Cairn Geldie, where it remains to this day. Over the years, many men have tried to locate the treasure from the Tree of Gold.

Wormy Hillock Henge

Wormy Hillock Henge is a small henge in Clashindarroch Forest near Huntly. It is a low circular bank, 54ft in diameter, which almost encircles a 20ft wide platform in the centre. There is a single gap in the bank at the south-east end of the henge. According to legend, the henge was the site of a buried dragon. As it was told, this dragon had been attacking villages in the area, and the people eventually managed to kill it. They half-buried its carcass and flung dirt over it, making a mound. A large boulder lies in the ditch directly below one of the pits found there. At the time of writing, the henge is overgrown with heather and grass.

THE TRICK

I have told this story many times over the past few years. It is my own creation, based on an old Yugoslavian tale that I have greatly enjoyed, and decided I could bring into a Scottish setting. I have always loved trickster tales, and I find this one very satisfying. – G.B.

Eddie was fed up. The van's rear door was not high enough to shelter him from the driving rain, and he had forgotten his golf brolly. The rain had run down inside his collar, and his skin was soaking. His clothes were damp, and he was chilled to the marrow.

He was at the Thainstone Mart by Inverurie for the Sunday car boot sale. On a good day, his fruit and vegetables might have sold by eleven o'clock. It was now half an hour after this, and he had sold nothing. He had been forced to leave the trays in the van for protection from the rain, and with nothing on display, people were not stopping by. In fact, there were few people going about at all. Those who were, hurriedly visited only the vehicles they knew would have what they wanted.

There were no browsers today.

Yesterday Eddie had been so excited. 'Ruth, the morn, whatever I sell at the car boot will be towards yer birthday!'

Eddie shivered and frowned. This was rubbish! He would just have to come back next week. His daughter Ruth's twenty-first was not for another three weeks yet, and he was determined to make it something special. For now, though, he just needed to pack up and get home. The thought of a nice hot soak was very appealing.

The car park had been very quiet all day, but just then, Eddie noticed a beautiful silver Daimler enter. It rolled over the muddy ground to come to a standstill as close to the entrance as was possible. Intrigued, Eddie forgot about his numb fingers and dripping nose, and watched the driver's door open.

A tall man stepped out, dressed in a full-length Italian coat, with a hat perched jauntily on his head, and on his feet, Italian leather boots. The man strolled into the market area, apparently ignoring the foul weather. He began to strut around the cars, regarding them all as if he owned the lot.

Eddie was just about to close up the van when he heard the man's measured footsteps stop behind him. 'Any joy the day?'

Eddie turned round, and found he had to crane his neck in order to look up to see the man's face. He was smiling at Eddie, amusement in his eyes.

'I've selt nothin! Abody's jist rushin on!'

The man nodded sympathetically, then as if a sudden idea had crossed his mind, he said, 'Well, how much wid ye be willin tae sell yer wares for?' He bent forward and peered into the back of Eddie's van.

'Fit d'ye mean?'

'I'm askin, how much are ye willin tae sell the whole lot for, everything I can see?' Eddie's face broke into a smile, the rain forgotten. 'Ye want tae buy a' ma produce?'

'That's what I'm askin.'

Eddie stroked his beard and looked at the man carefully. 'Two hundred and fifty quid.'

'That's for everything I can see?'

'Aye! Grand, where shall I pit the trays, then?'

The man looked shocked. 'Did ye no see the car I arrived in?'

'Aye, it's richt smart!'

'Well, I'll no be carryin yer trays in the back o' it! Ye'll hae tae follow me hame.'

'Oh, aright, then. Lead on, Macduff!'

The man gave him a distasteful look and stalked back to his car. Eddie slammed the boot shut, and gratefully climbed into his van.

He followed the Daimler as it headed out of the car park and took a right turn. Eddie's van was not the most modern of vehicles, but she was reliable and he had no problem keeping up with the man in front. Fifteen minutes later, he found himself on a road he didn't know. He continued to follow the Daimler as it indicated left and headed up a well-kept drive lined with bushes and trees. The road curved round, and opened out before a large mansion, gleaming white in the fading light.

Eddie drew up behind the silver car, but the man got out and gestured for him to reverse down the side of the house.

'Yes, sir!' muttered Eddie, shifting gear.

Once he had parked at the side of the house, Eddie opened up the doors to haul out the trays of fruit and vegetables.

'What d'ye think yer doin?' shouted the man, as he stalked up to Eddie.

'I'm emptying the van!'

'No yer nae!'

'What? Ye don't want tae buy the veggies noo?' Eddie was getting a tad impatient, and he shivered, cold to the bones. 'Yes, I'm buyin the lot from ye and I get yer van too.'

'Pardon?'

'I asked if I could have everythin I could see for the two hundred and fifty pounds, and you said yes.' Eddie was speechless. This guy was unreal.

'I nivver said ye could have ma van! That's ridiculous!'

'Well, we can tak it tae court if ye like.'

The following day, Eddie and Mr Gray, for that was the man's name, met at the courts.

When the judge had heard their accounts, he cleared his throat and said, 'Mr Gray, if those were your exact words, Mr Smith is indeed obliged to give you his van.'

Mr Gray smiled at Eddie, and took out his wallet. 'So, Mr Smith, here's yer two fifty, and I'll tak the keys tae ma van, if ye please.' He held out his hand, and Eddie numbly handed them over.

It took two buses and a mile's walk for Eddie to get back home. When he walked in, Ruth was seated at the kitchen table. 'Well?' she asked. Eddie shook his head and sat down heavily on one of the chairs, his jacket still on. Ruth got up and put the kettle on.

'Och, Dad, what a chancer!'

'Aye, but ain who kens a thing or two!' he said bitterly. 'That money'll have tae go tae a new van, love, nae yer birthday!' Ruth smiled. 'Don't worry, Dad. I'll go tae the mart this Sunday, and I'll sell the produce.'

'With what? The van's gone!'

'Aye, but there's still Squeaky,' she countered.

'Squeaky? The VW.? No way! She won't run!'

'I bet she will, Dad! Ye know I love drivin her!'

The following Sunday, Ruth filled up the tattered green van with all the trays. It was a lovely day, the sun bright in a blue sky.

'Noo watch out for that cratur if he's there again!'

Ruth nodded and grinned, her cheeks dimpling. 'I can look aifter masel, Dad!' Eddie grinned back. 'Aye, I ken, it should be Mr Gray that looks out!'

At the mart, it did not take Ruth long to set up the trays in an attractive manner, the colours of the fruit and vegetables blending pleasingly. Custom arrived early on such a fine day, and soon Ruth was doing brisk trade.

At one point, she happened to look up, and there stood a man dressed in a long Italian coat, with a hat and boots like her dad had described. He smiled at her in a friendly way. 'Mornin'. How's sales?' 'Fine, thanks,' Ruth replied, smiling back, 'would ye like anythin?'

'How much wid it be for everythin I can see?'

Ruth raised her eyebrows. 'Everythin?' 'That's richt.'

'Well …' She looked at what she had left and frowned as if calculating. 'Five hundred and fifty pounds.'

Mr Gray nodded. 'Very well, I'll buy the lot! But ye'll have tae drive the goods tae ma hoose. I don't have room in my car.'

'Okay, but I'd like tae see the colour o' yer money first,' said Ruth.

The man looked surprised, but grinned and fished out his wallet. He counted out the notes and held them up for Ruth to inspect.

'So, I get everything I can see, an you do as well?'

'Yes!'

She nodded, satisfied. 'Fine! Lead on, I'll follow.'

Arriving at the mansion, Ruth reversed around the side of the house. She hopped out of the van, and waited calmly as Mr Gray approached. His feet crunched on the chuckies and as he walked, he took out his wallet, once again counting out the money. 'There ye go. Five hundred an' fifty pounds for all the food, an' I take the van as well.' He smiled triumphantly, but Ruth was nonplussed.

'Thank you,' she said, 'but that's not all ye owe me.'

'What d'ye mean?'

'When ye showed me yer money earlier, I asked if I get everything I can see, and you said yes. That includes yer wrist, and the hand ye held the notes in.'

Mr Gray forced a laugh, but looked irritated. 'That's daft! I'm no giving ye ma hand and wrist! That's just plain stupid!'

Ruth remained very calm. 'Is it, Mr Gray? Let's see what the courts say.'

When the judge had heard their story, he was silent for a time. He had dealt with Mr Gray many times before and had benefitted hugely from it, but this time he was flummoxed. Miss Smith had him over a barrel.

'Well, Miss Smith has a point, Mr Gray. Obviously you cannot give her your hand and wrist, but perhaps you can give her something of their value?'

Mr Gray had tried to stay reasonable. He had never been beaten at his own game, but he could feel his rage begin to sing.

'How much?' he snarled.

'I think two thousand pounds would be a fair exchange. Miss Smith, would you agree to this amount?'

Ruth nodded, her face solemn, but her eyes gleeful. Mr Gray could contain himself no longer.

'You … you … young whippersnapper!' he spat. 'Ye think ye've beaten me! But I'll show ye! A … a … a … wager! If I can tell a better lie than you, ye tak the five fifty an' be done wi' it. If ye tell a better lie than I, ye can have the two grand and … anither two grand on top!'

The judge stammered. 'Mr Gray, are you sure …'

But the man was beyond reasoning. 'You will judge which is the better lie, yer Honour!' He winked at the judge, who swallowed nervously and nodded.

'I will begin!' declared Mr Gray bullishly. 'Some time ago, while I was sleeping, I threw three seed grains out of my window, and immediately a field of green wheat grew up, healthy and strong. Ten of my sheep got into that field and disappeared, and though my men searched high and low for them, they were never found.

'When it came to the hairst, the wheat was harvested, and the first loaf of bread to be made was placed on my breakfast table. I buttered a slice, and ate it, and as I did, a sheep the size of a deerhound came out of my mouth! The next bite a sheep the size of a small cow came forth, followed by one the size of a bull!

'Every sheep was bigger than the last, and I was able to sell those beasts for a very large sum, and so became a very wealthy man!' Mr Gray was very pleased with his tale. 'Now, young lady, I'll bet ye can't do better!'

Ruth smiled and began. 'I too threw three seeds from my window, but they were lavender seeds, and where they fell, a mighty bush grew up overnight. The shadow from this bush stretched for three whole days' walking!

'Well, when the lavender came into bloom, I picked the flowers, and from them I made the choicest of perfume oils. I sold these oils for a great price, and with the income, I invested in three merchant ships, which I loaded with goods to sell abroad.

'My brother kindly took charge of the vessels, but ...' and she hesitated, her voice breaking. 'That was three years ago ... pirates attacked my ships, stole all my merchandise and ... killed my brother.' She stopped, her face downcast, her hands twisting in mock distress. Then she said quietly, 'The day my brother left, he was wearing the very coat that you have on, Mr Gray.' Ruth suddenly looked up, her eyes burning. 'You were that pirate, Mr Gray. It was you who killed my brother!'

There was a stunned silence. The judge felt a great tension within the room. If he declared Mr Gray's story to be the better lie, then he declared Miss Smith's tale to be true, in which case, Mr Gray stood accused of murder and piracy. If he declared Miss Smith to have won, Mr Gray would be taken severely out of pocket. But to the judge's relief, the decision was taken out of his hands.

A torrent of rage cascaded from Mr Gray's lips, his face puce with anger. 'You LIAR! How DARE you accuse ME in such a way! I have NEVER been a pirate, and I have never even MET your brother!'

Shaking with emotion, he tore the coat from his back, and threw it down in front of Ruth. 'Have my coat! I don't want it! And ...' He took out his wallet, and with trembling fingers, counted out all the money he owed and slammed it down on top of his discarded coat.

Ruth silently held out the VW. keys, which Mr Gray swiped from her hand, and he stalked out of the room without looking back.

She looked enquiringly at the dazed judge, who shrugged and left. Ruth allowed a smile to break out on her face as she knelt down and gathered up her winnings, rolling them up and placing them in the pockets of the coat, which she then placed in a plastic bag.

Ruth made the journey home. As she entered the kitchen, Eddie looked up from his paper. 'Well?'

Ruth sighed, and lifted up the bag. She pulled out the coat, laying it on the table. 'He gave me this.' Eddie looked grim and shook his head. 'I dinna want tae see that coat, lass.'

'Maybe ye should just check the pockets.' Ruth could not keep the laughter out of her voice, and suddenly she was giggling.

Eddie smiled. 'What? What is it, Ruth?' She just pointed at the coat, tears running down her cheeks as she laughed.

Her dad got up and shoved his hand into one of the coat pockets. When he withdrew a roll of notes, he was stunned; his face was a picture, causing Ruth to burst out giggling again.

As you can well imagine, Ruth had a most wonderful birthday, and there was enough left over to buy a good van for Eddie's business. However, it must be said that Mr Gray and his Daimler were never seen again at the Inverurie car boot sale!

3

CASTLES

FRENCH KATE

From 1925 to 1965 my aunt, Mrs Helen Strachan, ran her bus service from Aberdeen to Braemar, along both the North and South Deeside roads. It ferried coffins, livestock, climbers, hikers, and tourists. During the war, a party of Canadian lumberjacks squeezed into the boot of the bus, to share the space with a crate of bantams and two old bikes, to get to a local dance through a blizzard. My father, Charles Middleton, was her manager, and her daughters, brothers, sisters and nephews etc. were variously employed as clippies and drivers. When the business ended, Pipe Major Norman Meldrum of Invercauld led a procession of forty buses and 200 people out of Braemar to close a chapter of

Deeside's history. A main part of the summer trade was composed of day trips up nearby glens, with the driver telling passengers the local legends. A big hit was always the story of French Kate. – S.B.

> Bonnie lassie, will ye go, will ye go, will ye go
> Bonnie lassie, will ye go to the birks o' Abergeldie?
> Ye shall get a gown o' silk, a gown o' silk a gown o' silk
> Ye shall get a gown o' silk an a coat o' calliemankie.

Craig nam Ban, or the hill of the woman, near Abergeldie, is covered with magnificent birch and oak woods, and has in its side a cave where once a Pictish chief hid when his men were defeated and his tribe was scattered. The castle of Abergeldie sits on the south side of the Dee, and is rich with bartizans, sculptures and turrets, alongside a clock with a bell striking the hour. It is a sixteenth-century tower house, built by the Gordons in 1550. Birch wine was once brewed here in abundance, as well as whisky, in the many illicit stills around the area.

When King George VI and his brother Bertie (King Edward VIII) stayed in the castle, they thought that the tower, infested by bats, was haunted by the ghost of a young witch burned to death locally. It is a fact that the commissioners appointed for the trial of witches on 6 April 1597 ordered that the Laird of Abergeldie be 'charged for the compearance before them at Aberdeen of Janet Guissett, accused of witchcraft'. However, this is not the witch that haunts the tower, but rather the young, ill-fated *Caitir Fhrangach* or French Kate, otherwise known as Kitty Rankine, a young French girl who acted as maid to the Lady Gordon. There are Rankines to this day living on Deeside, so the name lived on after the girl's death.

The tale is an old one, easily told. The lord of the castle was away in France on business, and his lady was lonely and jealous. As women have done since time immemorial, she turned to the Black Arts to see if she could divine whether or not her husband was remaining faithful to her on his long journey away from home. Kitty Rankine, her maid, was a noted practitioner of the soothsayer's skills. The lady decided to avail herself of Kitty's abilities.

The girl was taken before her mistress, and told to use her power to reveal how the lord of the castle was spending his time. She peered into a magic mirror, obscured by mist. At a word from her, the mist cleared, and the Lady Gordon could clearly see her husband wooing a young and attractive French woman on his way home from France.

'Is this how my lord treats me? You have the means to strike him down. Drown the wretch!' cried the lady.

And so, Kitty Rankine had a huge cauldron taken to the top of the castle to be filled with water, and an empty wooden bowl set floating on it, like a gallant ship on the sea. Down went the young witch, down to the castle cellar, and there she began to incant a spell for raising a storm. Kitty could control wind, rain, thunder and lightning using the magic she had learned. First, she dug a hole in the earth of the cellar, poured a little water in it, and cutting a strand of her long fair hair, stirred it into the mud, widdershins.

Round and round the wind I mix
Shake a boat with eildritch tricks
Bring a storm to all on board
Let it founder, ship and lord.

Away up in the tower, the water in the cauldron began to shiver. Waves appeared on the surface and the wooden bowl began to rock unsteadily. As Kitty's chanting grew louder, the waves in the bowl grew higher and higher. Soon, the wooden bowl was being flung about like seeds in a sieve.

All this time, the Lady Gordon looked on, tight-lipped. The water leaped up and down wildly in the cauldron, spilling and splashing over the sides. Then the wooden bowl was swamped by a large wave, and sank.

'As in the cauldron, so at sea,' Kitty told her mistress. 'Your husband's drowned, along with his fancy woman.'

The lady began to hope that Kitty Rankine's powers were not so strong. Perhaps her husband was safe after all. But then word came to the castle that the Lord of Abergeldie had been drowned in a terrible storm, which had whipped up from nowhere. None survived.

Now that the Lady of Abergeldie was a widow, she grew anxious that folk in the area would lay blame at her door. She condemned Kitty Rankine as a witch, and claimed the girl had acted out of malice against the family. Robert McKeiry, the wizard, was set on her trail. Immediately, she changed herself into a hare:

> I shall go into a hare,
> With sorrow and sych and meickle care.
> And I shall go in the Devil's name,
> Ay while I come home again.

But Robert McKeiry changed himself into a hound, until she cried out:

> Hare, hare, God send thee care.
> I am in a hare's likeness now,
> But I shall be in a woman's likeness even now.

And from a hare to a woman, she changed herself into a mouse. But Robert McKeiry changed himself into a weasel and caught her by the tail. Wriggle as she might, he was more powerful than her, and she was forced to change into her human form.

They led her before the sheriff, and the verdict of guilty was swift. Caitir Fhrangach was taken, trussed like a roast, to the summit of Craig nam Ban, and there she was burned at the stake. To this day, men claim to hear her ghostly death screams echoing over the dark waters of the Dee.

Alison Cross

The text given below originally appeared in Robert Jamieson's Popular
Ballads & Songs *2, published in 1806 pp.187–190, said to have
been collected from Mrs Anna Brown of Falkland, Aberdeen, the only
entry from the oral tradition.*

*The song was recorded by Peter Hall at the Jeannie Robertson
Memorial Concert in 1977, the last three verses coming from another
recording made by Tim Neat. – S.B.*

Aul Alison Gross she lives in yon tower,
The ugliest witch in the north country,
Has trysted me ae day til her bower
And many a braw speech she's made to me

Awa, awa, ye ugly witch, Haud far awa' an lat me be.
Afore I kiss your ugly mou
I'd raither toddle around the tree

She showed me a mantle of reid scarlet
Wrocht wi' golden fringes fine.
'Gin ye will be my leman so true,
This goodly gift it sall be thine'.

She showed me a sark o' the saftest silk,
Weel wrocht wi' pearls aboun the band.
'Gin ye will be my leman so true,
This goodly gift at yer command.'

She showed me a cup o' the guid red gowd
Weel set wi' jewels and they're sae fine.
'Gin ye will be my leman so true,
This goodly gift it shall be thine.'

She's taen oot her grass green horn,
She's blew it three times loud and shrill,

Swore by the moon and stars aboun
She'd gar me rue the day that I was born.

She's taen oot her silver wand,
She's turned three times aroun the tree,
Muttered sic words that my sense did fail
And I fell doon senseless tae the ground.

Wi silver basin an silver kaim
Tae kaim my headie upon her knee,
Aye on ilka Saturday nicht
Aul Alison Gross she comes tae me.

But it fell upon last Halloween
When the Seily Court cam ridin by,
The Queen's lichted on a gowan bank,
Nae far frae the tree where I did lie.

She's lifted me in her milk-white hand.
She's pricked me three times on her knee.
She's turned me back tae ma proper shape.
Nae mair I'll toddle aroon the tree.

The Plague Castle

I first heard this tale many years ago from my aunt Nancy Mackintosh at East Mains, Aboyne. Nancy was born in Carr Cottage in Glen Ey, and was raised both there and at Dee View Cottage, Corriemulzie, above Braemar. She was related to the Lamont family, who provided much material about the area gathered by Frances Diack from Kitty Calum of Glen Ey. The plague song comes from Stanley Robertson. – S.B.

Ding dong the Catholic bells
Mary is my mother
Bury me over in the old churchyard
Beside my eldest brother

My coffin shall be black
Six angels at my back
Two to preach and two to pray
And two to carry my soul away.

Centuries ago when the dreaded plague was raging, the clachan of Auchendryne held to the Catholic faith. The ancient castle of Ceann-Drochaide or Kyndrochit, as it came to be known, was infected with this disease. Folk called it the Galar Mòr, the great disease, and it was merciless wherever it went. The symptoms were horrific. Victims endured painful swellings of the lymph nodes, which turned black. They suffered from high fever, became delirious and finally vomited blood. Many died within two days of catching the illness, which obliterated entire communities. Such was the high death count that the Pope agreed victims could make their final confessions 'even to a woman' as there were too few priests left alive who could administer last rites.

It was feared that if people were suspected of being infected by the plague, their own neighbours and kinsmen would quarantine them in their houses, nailing up the windows and doors and leaving them to their fate.

Now when the Galar Mòr came to Kyndrochit Castle, it was not the ruin that stands in Braemar today. It was a sturdy keep, befitting the ancient lodge of the old Scots kings. A company of artillery tramped over from Athol, over the Cairnwell and on to Corriemulzie. On they went down Cor-nam-muc and set up their cannon at Dalvreckachy. Folk say that the beautiful queen of Kyndrochit was combing her lovely hair by her window when the first withering shots reduced the walls around her to rubble. No one escaped alive. The castle ruin lay like a place accursed, avoided by all.

Years passed. In the mid-eighteenth century, the plague was a distant memory, but the area around Braemar was again a centre of anxiety. Braemar Castle, seat of Clan Farquharson, was renovated for use as a barracks by Redcoat soldiers, after being leased to the Hanoverian Government by John Farquharson of Invercauld. The Redcoats were stationed there to ensure peace in the region after the ill-fated Jacobite Uprising of 1745. Ensign B. Sullivan and Corporal William Dix cut their names into the walls there; others scratched and scribbled on the window shutters of the drawing room. Time hung heavy on the soldiers' hands. The folk of the region, all Gaelic speakers, hated them as oppressors. Sometimes, the Redcoats must have wished they had the power of the old Clan chiefs, 'the power of pit and gallows', to hang or imprison the more militant among the population.

Their comrades were stationed at Dubrach, patrolling south-east into the hills over Glen Christie and Glen Connie to Glen Ey. Sergeant Arthur Davies, of Guise's regiment, was there, it being his duty to patrol the remote moors. He carried a purse with fifteen and a half gold guineas in it. Having gone off on a day's hunting, he simply seemed to vanish into thin air; until, that is, his ring appeared on the finger of a local man's girlfriend. A witness from Inverey claimed to have had a vision of the ghost of Sergeant Davies asking him to go to Glen Ey and bury his bones. There he had found the remains of the Redcoat sergeant. In court, the witness said that the ghost spoke in Gaelic, but the case was dismissed, as the Englishman did not speak the language. No one was prosecuted for the sergeant's murder, but tensions ran high between the Redcoats and the Aberdeenshire Highlanders.

One day, a carter delivering food to the barracks stayed for a game of cards with two of the soldiers. The older of the Redcoats was a gambler. The carter told him the tale of the ruined castle at Kyndrochit, and hinted at great treasure there, but made no mention of the plague. Jokingly, he bet the soldier a cask of heather ale that he would not dare climb down into the ruins and spend a night there. The ploy turned serious though, when the Redcoat accepted the challenge.

The next afternoon, after his turn of duty was done, the soldier arrived at the ruins of the ancient castle and dropped a stone down through a chink in the cairn. He could hear it rattling as if it were bouncing down a set of stairs into the depths. Not wishing to share the supposed treasure with any of his friends, he had gone alone, armed only with a rope. He proceeded to tie this to a nearby fir tree, before clearing a small hole large enough to wriggle through. Hand over hand, he lowered himself into the dark bowels of the ruin.

To his complete surprise there were entire vaults below the ruins, and a subterranean passage leading off to the Cluny from the old castle stables. There, in the event of a siege, horses could be watered from the river without leaving the castle itself. He dimly made things out with the aid of a strange light issuing from a door. Cautiously proceeding, he pushed ajar the creaking door and entered a room lit by ghostly wax candles. In the middle of the room was a table, and around that table sat a company of the dead. Each heart had stopped instantly with the first blast of the cannon. At its head sat a long dead chief, fierce in furs and armour, his long grey hair a tangle of dust and cobwebs. Time had stopped here like a broken clock. To his left was a beautiful lady, with eyes of deepest jade, one delicate hand frozen on her silk dress, her long lace petticoats nibbled away by rats. Beside her knelt a servant, and an open chest of coins, as if preparing with his mistress to flee. Courtiers slumped around the table, skull eye sockets empty of all but the musty gloom.

The Redcoat took one frightened step closer to the chest of gold. Something made him turn, and he glanced up at the face of a clansman, long dead of the plague. Terrified near to insanity, he scrambled from the room, squeezing himself up the crumbling stair until with a hard yank on the rope, he was once more free of the ruins. By now the moon was rising, a clear and cloudless night lighting the road.

On his way back to the barracks, a queer little figure stepped from the bushes by the road and accosted him; a dwarf wearing a greasy red cap. He cocked his head sideways, shuffled before the soldier and tugged at his sleeves. He warned him, if he valued his life, to tell no one what he had seen in the Castle of Ceann-Drochaide. However there was little need of a warning. Soon afterwards the soldier requested a transfer and went to fight in a foreign war, where he died, taking his secret with him. To this day the castle remains an enigma. Even my aunt, Nancy Mackintosh of Corriemulzie, went to her grave without learning all the castle's secrets, so I know as little of the truth of the legend as the grey stones of the Lion's Face at Invercauld. For all I know, the ghostly sitters may circle that table yet.

THE SMITH OF KILDRUMMY CASTLE

This story always revives memories of dried pee, warm milk and chalk; in fact of Mile End Primary School in the 1950s. The highlight of my school week came when the teacher switched on the wireless, and turned the knob to the Scottish History programme. One poor soul by the name of Campbell had a dreadful playtime after we were treated to the Massacre of Glencoe. The crunch of Kate Barlass' arm as it shattered when the king's enemies smashed the door open produced a wonderful shiver of fright, but even Mary Queen of Scots' head dropping off was as nothing to the following story for sheer blood curdling horror. – S.B.

This story concerns the siege of the castle at Kildrummy during the bloody Scottish Wars of Independence. Kildrummy at the time was surrounded by an 85ft wide moat. At the tops of the walls and towers were wooden hoardings from which archers could easily defend the outer walls. They were also used as a platform from which boiling oil, stones, and excrement could be lobbed down on attackers below. This forbidding fortress was built on a low hilltop, and its Snow Tower had a well in the basement. There was also a sunken passage down to the stream at the bottom of the Back Den, a tunnel with stone steps grassed over to hide it from view. The castle also had latrine chutes, carefully designed to prevent any invader from scaling them. Built by the Earl of Mar, it had a magnificent great hall with a minstrels' balcony, a chapel, prison, bakery and brewhouse. Its interior walls were plastered, and covered in gorgeous hangings. There were sweet-smelling rushes on the floors, and silver plates for entertaining royalty. There was all this and more, but little did the folk within the castle know of the fate that was to befall it.

Nearby the castle, on the southern slopes of Ben Newe, at a small farmstead called Greenstyle, lived a family known at that time by the name of Osbarn. There were three sons in the family, and the eldest was known as Osbarn the Smith, that being his trade. The family was ill-liked in the area, for they were all mean and greedy by nature. He was lucky enough to be hired to work at the castle, as there was always a large garrison of soldiers there. He was kept busy shoeing horses, repairing weapons and armour, forging hinges and iron gates, as well as constructing farming tools. He was well paid, and lived in comparative comfort within Kildrummy. However, he had no loyalties, no morals and no friends.

Summer came. It was the year of 1306. King Robert the Bruce had been defeated near Perth, and had gone to ground before travelling to Aberdeen, where his brother Nigel Bruce, his queen and his daughter Marjorie joined him. The womenfolk were unable to contend with the constant dangers of the campaign, and Bruce sent them to Kildrummy Castle, escorted by his brother Nigel and the Earl of Atholl.

A great feast was prepared at Kildrummy for the royal party. Marjorie, the king's sister Marie, his brother Nigel, the Countess

of Buchan and the Earl of Atholl arrived, together with many Scottish nobles. But their respite was not to last. Edward of Caernarvon, Prince of Wales, son of Edward I (the 'Hammer of the Scots'), was marching north. Hurriedly the royal womenfolk fled to the sanctuary of St Duthac's Chapel at Tain. Nigel Bruce, however, stayed at Kildrummy to face the English invaders.

The castle made ready for a long siege. Food and ammunition were assembled in the great hall, the wooden wall-hoardings were manned, the gatehouse was bolted, the iron gates were set in place and the drawbridge was raised. All was ready to withstand the worst that the English could inflict.

Edward of Caernarvon crossed the Mounth on the first day of August, flags flying and bridles jingling, and camped at Kildrummy. The English army's armour was magnificent. The knights' clothing was of the finest silk. The prince's battle flags were of beaten gold. With him, he took his falcons, and entertained himself by hawking, netting partridges, playing dice, and watching his court fool. A lion was also a part of his entourage.

His opponent Nigel Bruce was a man of tremendous courage, and roused the men to repel the furious attacks made by the English. But the days turned to weeks, and provisions dropped lower and lower. Osbarn the Smith began to consider his options. If the English took the castle, everyone, himself included, would be slaughtered. Realistically, the castle was doomed to fall.

At last, Osbarn knew what he wanted to do. He would creep from the castle under cover of darkness, cross the enemy lines, and offer to betray his countrymen in any way he could, for a reward, of course. Beneath a clouded moon, he removed some stones from behind the smiddy at the castle wall, crawled over the rough ground and surrendered to the English sentries, asking to be taken to the prince's tent.

Here, he explained the nature of his mission, and named his price for helping the English: a sack of gold. No one likes a turncoat. He might have come as a spy. Could a traitor be trusted? Eventually they came to an agreement. At a predetermined signal from the English, the smith was to set fire to the castle. In return, the prince promised that he would have as much gold as he could carry. Osbarn was built like a barn door! He would be rich beyond his wildest dreams.

He returned to the castle before daylight, blocked up the hole he had crawled through, and went immediately to his forge. It was near to the great hall, which was thatched and roofed with wood. Easy enough to toss a red-hot horseshoe onto the roof, once the signal was given. And then, it came. He flung the metal up, and the thatch set alight instantly. The fire spread too fast to be extinguished. Now, the English attacked. But Nigel Bruce and his followers rebuilt the walls that had been breached by fire during the night.

However, valuable stores had been burned. It was starvation that made Sir Nigel Bruce surrender, not loss of courage nor military defeat. In September, the castle was handed over to Edward of Caernarvon. The Bruce's brother was taken prisoner and hanged at Berwick, and the garrison all massacred. All, that is, except for Osbarn the Smith.

The blacksmith turned up jauntily at the English camp, demanding gold for his treachery. Prince Edward smiled, and ordered the gold to be brought before him. Osbarn was bound hand and foot. The gold was melted on his own forge. The soldiers grabbed his hair, and pulled back his head, whereupon the molten gold was poured down his throat, perhaps the most suitably treacherous end for a traitor.

Before the siege, the queen, Princess Marjory, the Bruce's sisters, and others of the royal party had sought refuge at Tain. They were now surrendered to the English, and taken to England to be displayed in cages. Sir Nigel Bruce was brought with his knights to Berwick, there to be hanged, drawn, and beheaded: one of the bravest men in the kingdom.

The Baron o' Braichlie

You will find a Scots version of this on the Elphinstone Kist section of the University of Aberdeen's website, under the section 'Stories for Bairns' by Les Wheeler. Carn na cuimhne, the Farquharsons' muster Cairn of Remembrance, is a short hop over a dyke, and lies between the main Deeside Road and the Dee. The present Chieftain of the Ballater Highland Games is Captain Alwyn A.C. Farquharson M.C. of Invercauld. His appointment was duly confirmed at a public meeting of the Games held on 24 November 1948, and he has now completed sixty-two years in this post. Captain Farquharson is the 16th Chief of the Clan Farquharson, and can trace his lineage back to Farquhar, 4th son of Alexander Ciar (Shaw) Mackintosh of Rothiemurchus (1411–1492). – S.B.

On 7 September 1666, Iain Farquharson, clan chief of the Inverey Farquharsons, killed Baron Gordon of Braichlie over a long-running property dispute. The Gordon version appears in the old ballad 'The Baron o' Braichlie':

> Doon Deeside came Inverey, whistlin' and playin'
> He's lichted at Braichlie's yett at the day dawin
> Says, 'Baron o' Braichlie, it's are ye within?
> There's sharp swords at your yett will gar your blood spin.'

> Up spake the proud baron o'er the castle wa'
> 'Are ye come to spoil or plunder my ha'?
> Or gin ye be gentlemen, licht and come in
> Gin ye drink o' my wine ye'll no gar my blood spin.'

> His lady rose up, to the window she went
> She heard her kye lowin o'er hill and o'er fen
> 'Oh, rise up, bold, Braichlie and turn back your kye
> The lads o' Drumwharren are drivin them by!'

'How can I rise, lady, and turn them again?
For whaur I hae ae man I'd lief to hae ten.'
She called on her Marys to come to her hand
Says, 'Bring your rocks, lasses, we will them command.'

'Gin I had a husband as I wot I hae nane
He'd no be in his bed and see his kye taen.'
'Now haud your tongue, Peggy, and gie me my gun
Ye'll see me gang oot, but I'll never come in.'

'Arise, Betsy Gordon, and gie me my gun
I will gang oot though I never come in
Then kiss me, my Peggy, I'll no longer stay
For I will gang oot and I'll meet Inverey.'

When Braichlie was ready and stood in the close
A bonnier callant ne'er mounted a horse
'What'll come o' your lady and your bonnie young son?
Oh, what'll come o' them when is gane?'

'Strike dogs,' cries Inverey, 'fecht till you're slain
For we are four hundred and ye are four men!
'Strike, strike, ye proud boaster, your honour is gane
Your lands we will plunder and your castle we'll burn!'

At the head o' the Etnach the battle began
At little Auchoilzie they killed the first man
First they killed ae man and syne they killed twa
And they killed gallant, Braichlie the flower o' them a'.

'Came ye by Braichlie s yetts, came ye by there?
And saw ye his Peggy a-tearing her hair?'
'Oh, it's I came by Braichlie's yells, I came by there
And I saw Peggy Gordon a-braidin her hair.'

'She was ranting and dancin' and singin' for joy
She swore that ere nicht she would feast Inverey
She ate wi' him, drank wi' him, welcomed him in
She was kind to the man that had slain her baron.'

'Oh, fie on ye, lady, why did ye dae sae
Ye opened yer yetts tae the fause Inverey.'
There's dule in the kitchen and mirth in the ha'
For the Baron o' Braichlie is dead and awa'.

A Gordon sympathiser wrote this ballad, for there is more than one side to the tale.

The Children of the Trough

The baron was on poor terms with his fellow Gordon down Deeside, the Lord of Aboyne. Folk say that Braichlie was a great fat brute who used to poach the Lord of Aboyne's salmon from

his stretch of the Dee. The lord's water bailiff was sent to Braichlie to tell him to stop this. The reply was as might have been expected, that Braichlie would fish where he liked.

However, the Lord of Aboyne was quite friendly with John, the Black Colonel of Inverey, the boldest of the Farquharson chieftains. He had a letter sent to him, suggesting that if John drove off Braichlie's cattle, he would let the Farquharsons' tenants cut peats from a Gordon moss on Easter Morven. John had no desire to stir up a feud between himself and Braichlie for the sake of a few peats, so he sent a letter to Braichlie saying that he intended to drive his cattle off on a specified day, to gain access to Lord Aboyne's peat moss, but promising to return the herd within the week.

Inverey's ploy failed. Braichlie resisted the driving off of his herd, and was killed doing so. Many thought that the young Colonel of Inverey had right on his side. However, as might be expected, the Marquis of Huntly, great chief of the Gordons, decided to punish the insult to his clan, and rode into Deeside alongside his allies Clan Grant. The Earl of Huntly, known as the Cock o' the North, was Crown Administrator for the lands of the Earldom of Mar at that time. No warning was given of their arrival, for had it been given, the fiery cross (the Croistarich) would have summoned Clan Chattan to confront them, the Farquharsons being a part of that great confederacy.

The cross was wood, half-burnt and dipped in blood, in token of the revenge by fire and sword to be carried out on those clansmen who did not answer the summons. Passed from one messenger to another, the alarm was spread across the districts of Mar in an incredibly short time.

The fiery cross would have brought clansmen hurrying to their muster spot at the bottom of Glen Feardar, *Carn na Cuimhne*, the Cairn of Remembrance. The custom was that each Farquharson going off to fight took a stone with him to the muster spot and placed it near to the cairn. If he survived the battle, he removed his stone. If he died, it was taken and added to the cairn, surrounded by its belt of larch and fir. The battle cry of the Farquharsons was '*Carn na Cuimhne*'.

Had the Farquarsons been warned that Huntly was bearing down on them, they would have raised the men of Glen Dee, Glen Ey, and the men of Corriemulzie, those from Glen Cluny, Auchindryne, and Balmoral.

But the Cock o' the North planned a stealthy and bloodthirsty attack, giving no chance for the enemy to prepare. Grant marched down from the upper reaches of the Dee, and Gordon attacked from the south. Crops and houses were burned, cattle stolen, men and women murdered. Only the children of the murdered Farquharson clan were taken prisoner by Huntly. Two hundred more orphaned children were captured by the Gordons, and carried off from Deeside to Huntly Castle. First though, the

Gordons and Grants visited Kyndrochit for a week's hunting, so noted was that place for a surfeit of game. And what a week they had of it!

Falconers, fowlers and fishers travelled with the earl, armed with hawks, longbows and forked arrows, swords, harquebuses, muskets, dirks, and Lochaber axes. They trapped many deer, wild horses, even wolves, whose heads were turned into sporrans. A kitchen was set up by the Cluny, kettles and pots boiling, spits turning, and venison baking. The invaders gorged themselves on roast beef and stewed mutton, on goats, kids, hares, fresh salmon, pigeons, hens, capons, chickens, partridges, moor coots, heathcocks, capercaillies and ptarmigans. They plundered the cellars of the Farquharson fallen for good ale, white wine, claret and whisky. Deer on Deeside were as numerous as bees in a byke – a man could stand for half an hour watching one huge herd cross a road – and the animals were easily stalked and rounded up in a tinchel. Then the earl would unleash his strong Irish greyhounds, and between those and the discharging of guns and arrows, and the slashing of dirks and daggers, the deer were quickly despatched. Kyndrochit was famed in all Scotland for the wealth of its game; in truth, a bountiful land.

Several months elapsed. The Chief of Clan Grant was invited for a week's stay at the great castle of the Cock o' the North. And what a welcome he had on the night he arrived! After the earl's fool and the minstrels had brought the evening to a conclusion, Gordon asked Grant if he would like to see some fun. The Laird of Grant agreed. To his bewilderment, his ally led him up to a balcony overlooking the kitchens. The cooks and kitchen boys were busily scraping the fatty scraps and gnawed bones from the plates that Grant and his men had just dined off into a long trough spanning the length of the kitchen.

'This is the best bit,' laughed the Cock o' the North. 'Endless fun.'

By now, the trough was full of the feast's leftovers. Raising a silver whistle to his lips, the head cook blew shrilly. A kitchen maid opened a hatch into the dungeons below, and up raced dozens of filthy, ragged, starving children, wild as wolves, who fed more like pigs than humans, fighting and tearing at each other for the greasy skin and lumps of fat from the evening's meal.

'I'll wager you never saw a funnier sight than that!' roared the earl. 'Those are the bairns of the Farquharsons we killed last year. What a hoot!' The Laird of Grant was horrified at the treatment of the orphans, and tried to come up with a way to save them without letting the Gordon brute think that he was soft-hearted.

'I helped create orphans of those bairns below, and you must be tired of them filling up your dungeon now. I'm sure you need it for fiercer villains. Let me take them with me so I can share the joke with my own folk.'

Huntly agreed. He was beginning to tire of them, and was thinking of having them killed anyway. When the Laird of Grant left, 200 verminous, starving children trailed and crawled behind him. Once clear of Gordon country, the Laird of Grant found homes for each one of them with his clansmen, where they were given the name of Grant. Even today, they are styled 'the Race of the Trough'.

Riddle Five

Older and wiser, yet young I may be
Drink twice of the riches that come from me

THE TAD-LOSGANN (THE TOAD-FROG)

Les Wheeler, the renowned editor, poet and north-eastern storyteller often tells this tale. Under the section 'Doric Verse' on the Elphinstone Institute website, you'll find 'The Beast of Kindrochit', where he has put it into Scots ballad form. On this site you will find more tales from the North-East that he has collected. – S.B.

If you travel to the Muir of Dinnet, you will see Loch Kinord. In its waters there is a small grassy hillock overrun by bushes and stones. Once upon a time this was the finest Iron Age crannog in all the North-East; from here there was a causeway over the loch to the shore. It is 2,000 years old and in the mud of its foundations, four hollowed-out log canoes have been found. This crannog was in use into the Middle Ages. It was a prison during the reign of Malcolm Canmore. The king and his second wife, Saint Margaret, often stayed in this island fortress.

But Malcolm most often stayed at the castle of Kyndrochit in Braemar. He kept in a pit there a huge creature called the Tad-Losgann, the toad-frog. Some said it was a monstrous boar of enormous size and ferocity, and some even thought it might be a crocodile, gifted to Malcolm by a foreign king. To feed this beast, the people around were taxed, each in turn, one of their cows or sheep in order to feed it. The pit where it was held was dug into the rocks of the river Cluny, on which the castle was built.

A few years before this beast arrived, a man by the name of Macleod married and had a son. His aged widowed mother lived further up the glen, and had only one milking cow to provide her with sustenance. The time came when it was her turn to feed the Kyndrochit monster. As the king's henchmen led away her only possession, she screamed out in grief and anger, '*Nach truagh nach eil a h-aon de shiol Thorcuill boo, a mharbhadh an Tad-Losgann!*' Which translates as, 'What a pity there is not one of the Siol Torquil alive to kill the Tad-Losgann!'

Well, the next day the Tad-Losgann was found slaughtered, an arrow impaled in one of its nasty yellow eyes. The king immediately ordered that a gallows be erected on the slopes of Craig Choinnich. His spies went into the countryside to find out who had killed the king's pet. It did not take them long to arrest the widow's son.

He was taken, bound by the hands, and led before the king who sat on a raised throne to pronounce judgement. Nobles and clansmen sat beside the king, fierce clan chiefs with grey deerhounds at their sides. Local crofters stood beside them, cowed and quiet. The death sentence was quickly pronounced, and just as the condemned man reached the foot of the gibbet a woman rushed forward weeping, her baby tied to her back in her plaid, and a toddler dogging her heels. She flung her arms around Macleod, begging the king to have mercy on her unfortunate husband.

She was dragged away by the guards, still sobbing, pleading that she be allowed to die with her husband. This display of loyalty and affection moved the king to pity. One of the king's favourite nobles, Allan Durward, remarked that it would be a shame to execute such a skilled archer.

King Malcolm considered this advice; he was always in need of good warriors. He therefore ordered that the prisoner be taken down to the Dee, along with his wife, baby, and infant son. The wife was sent off with the infant to stand between two firs, a distance away, and a fir cone was placed on the child's head.

'Now, Macleod,' said Malcolm, 'I order you to fire an arrow to split that fir cone. Do it, and your family walk free.'

Macleod requested three arrows, scrutinising each one carefully. He held the first between his teeth, the second he thrust into his belt, and the third he placed in the bow. His hands, as he did so, were shaking. His little son, thinking it was a game, was laughing and wriggling in his mother's arms. His wife was white with dread.

Very carefully, very reluctantly, he took aim. Then he pulled the bowstring. The arrow toppled the cone, his wife hugged their son and smothered the child in kisses.

The hill folk clapped and cheered, but King Malcolm was puzzled.

'You are a master archer,' he said. 'Why did you request three arrows?'

'If I had missed the cone and killed my wife or son, sire, I certainly would not have missed you,' came the bold response.

The king extended his hand in friendship, and offered Macleod a position as one of his bodyguards. But Macleod refused the honour.

'I could not love you enough to defend your life after such a test as you set for me,' he replied.

For once, the King was merciful. 'Hardy by nature, Hardy by name,' he decreed, 'now and hereafter.'

And to this day, the descendants of Macleod are called MacHardy. The family crest has four fierce boars in its quarters.

Hardi is the French for courageous.

The Laird o' Drum

This is a true story from a ballad I initially heard from the traveller John Watt Stewart. However, I never heard it sung with greater feeling and force than by the late Stanley Robertson, in the castle grounds themselves. The Robertsons were always treated with respect and kindness by the Lairds of Drum. I had originally researched the story for a series of proposed school visits to National Trust properties, arranged between the Trust and Aberdeen University's Elphinstone Institute, but the major part of the project foundered when, in 2001, a national outbreak of foot-and-mouth disease closed down all North-East farms for many months, and restricted movement around the countryside. – S.B.

Drum Castle is a sturdy rook-haunted keep, riddled with secret passages. The house was home to generations of Irvines from 1323 to 1975, having been gifted the land by King Robert the Bruce. According to family legend, the barony and the holly on the Irvine crest were awarded after William de Irwyn guarded the king, sleeping under a bush of the spiky plant. Within the castle, there are tables with pieces of wood carved out of them that allowed the portly lairds of the past extra room to sit. Some of the chambers are stained crimson red, said to be painted with pigs' blood. Much of the history of this castle, with its winding staircases, was concerned with hunting and battle. Outside, in the generous grounds, are damask and moss roses dating back to the sixteenth century. Scots roses flower abundantly, making good hedges alongside sweet briars. Turn a corner, and once you would have found a fish pond. The water came from a castle run-off, and drained into a rill, which led to Robbie Ross's Loch. Ancient horse chestnuts, lime and copper beech grow alongside mighty oaks where hawks soar in the pearly skies. To visit Drum is to step back into the mystery and romance of the past.

On the subject of romance, one fine morning, the Laird of Drum was hunting in the ancient forest, when he spied a young girl shearing barley in her father's field. He was so struck by her great beauty that he instantly proposed marriage, asking her to return with him to become the Lady of Drum. Her spirited reply surprised him. She refused to entertain his suit, saying that she was too lowborn to be a fitting wife for a laird, and would not consider becoming his mistress. However, she informed him that her father was an old shepherd, and that she was a dutiful daughter. This response made the laird even keener to possess her, hoping he could win the father's consent.

'If you set aside your plain grey gown, and agree to wear the silk and scarlet dress which I'll have made for you, I'll prove that my offer of marriage is genuine,' he urged.

'I wadna' feel richt in silken falderals, sir,' she replied. 'Plain lamb's wool suits me best.'

The laird was not to be so easily outdone. He rode across the hill till he found the shepherd, her father, and pressed him to give the match his blessing. The old man was as wary as his daughter, however, and pointed out the drawbacks to such a union.

'My dother's illiterate, sir, and never attended school. But she can milk cows and ewes, work in the barn, winnow corn, and aid the miller. She's trained tae saddle a horse, and pull on a gentleman's buits, but kens nothin o' genteel weys,' he confessed.

This had no effect in damping the laird's ardour.

'I'll teach the lassie to read and write myself, and there'll be no need for her to help to saddle my horse or pull on my boots,' he informed the old man.

The girl was still reluctant to agree, fearing a poor reception from his kinsmen.

'Fa'll bake ma bridal breid? And fa'll brew my ale? And fa is gaun tae welcome a poor shepherdess inside the michty waas o' Drum Castle?' she asked.

The laird brushed all her fears aside, took her up on his saddle, and sent word ahead that he was returning bearing a new bride. Twenty-four nobles stood at the gates of Drum Castle when they rode up. Not one doffed his hat as the new Lady of Drum passed by. The laird, however, more than made up for this dour reception. Taking her by the hand, he led her from room to room of the great castle.

'This is your home, now, my lady. And all this is your own,' he said gently.

His brother was furious. 'You've done the family of Drum a great wrong by this marriage,' he raged. 'She's a common shepherdess, a disgrace to mix her blood with that of a noble line like ours. This Peggy Coutts has bewitched you. I grant she's bonnie, and you haven't looks or youth in your favour … but a shepherd's daughter? Come, come, sir!'

Kittled, the laird retaliated. 'I've done nothing illegal nor immoral, brother. I've married a modest, hardworking lassie, whereas you are wed to a useless spendthrift.'

Turning round to address the company, he reminded them of his first wife.

'Have you forgotten so quickly what manner of marriage I had before? She was so high-born that I had to enter the room with my cap in my hand, bowing. Not only was she proud, she was avaricious. She wouldn't cross the threshold of Drum until I had loaded her down with pearls and precious jewels. All she loved was gold.'

Still the knights hung back at the gates of Drum, loath to welcome the young girl bride. The laird dismissed them with a wave of his hand, gave his bride the keys to the castle, and showered her with kisses. After the bridal feast, it was time for bed. The Laird of Drum and the shepherd's daughter lay down together as man and wife.

'Fan I am deid and ye are deid,' Peggy Coutts told her new husband, 'and we lie in the grave thegither, which ane o' yer prood nobles could tell oor dust apart?'

Despite all the odds, the marriage was a happy one. There are troubled spirits that walk the draughty passageways of Drum, but the laird and his child bride sleep quiet and undisturbed.

For his first wife, Alexander Irvine, Laird of Drum, married Lady Mary Gordon, daughter of the Marquis of Huntly and niece to the Marquis of Argyle on 7 December 1643. Drum is only 10 miles from Aberdeen off the Deeside road. In 1681 the Laird married as his second wife a sixteen-year-old shepherd girl called Peggy Coutts. Moreover, at the time the laird was sixty-three. Drum Castle was, from 1323 to 1975, the home of the Irvine family.

TIFTY'S ANNIE

This beautiful and tragic ballad was one I had heard dribs and drabs of over the years, but when Stanley Robertson sang it, I was very moved and asked him if he would teach me the song. I have fond memories of us both wandering around Old Aberdeen in the warm summer sunshine, as he was based at the Elphinstone Institute at the time. Stanley enthusiastically regaled me with tales and explanations surrounding the ballad.

One of his fondest stories was of when he had offered to take a group of men out to the woods of Fyvie and sing the song in situ. It was a pitch-dark night, and if I remember correctly, a wet one! But that never dissuaded Stanley. Near the site of Tifty's Mill he began to sing and, eerily, as he came to the verse where Andrew Lammie sounded his horn, the sound of a horn wafted up from the forest below. It was a hair-pricking-on-the-back-of-the-neck moment! Some of the group went down to investigate, but nobody was ever discovered ... – GB

At Mill o' Tifty there lived a man
In the neighbourhood o' Fyvie
And he had a lovely dochter fair
Her name wis bonnie Annie

Her look was like the springin' floor
That greets the rosy morning
Her innocence and precious mean
Her beauteous form adornin'

Lord Fyvie hed a trumpeter
His name wis Andrew Lammie
And he hed the airt for to gain the hert
O Tifty's Bonnie Annie

Lord Fyvie he cam ridin by
Far lived Bonnie Annie
And his trumpeter gaed on before
The bonnie Andrew Lammie

Her mother ca'ad her tae the door
'Cam here tae me ma Annie
Did ye ever see a prettier man
Than the trumpeter o' Fyvie?'

Naethin she said but sighed fu sair
Alas for Bonnie Annie
She durst not own that her hert wis won
By the trumpeter o' Fyvie

'When a love hes gone tae bed
And I lie my 'lane o'
Such loves oppress my tender breast
And love will waste my body.'

Wi' aipples sweet he did me treat
A' in the woods o' Fyvie
He ca'ad me mistress, but I said nane,
I am Tifty's Bonnie Annie.

Well Andrew would soond his trumpet shrill
'Yer cattle's lowin' Annie!'
And there they'd meet at the Brig o' Sleuch
At the Brig o' Sleuch near Fyvie.

Auld Tifty he cam ridin by
Saw Andrew wi' his Annie
And he was filled wi' a hatred sair
Taewards Andrew Lammie.

Fan Annie she cam hame that nicht
Her faither beat her cruelly
Her screams were heard o'er the castle wa'
And it brocht doon Lord Fyvie

'Why dae y beat yer dochter sair?
Why be cruel tae yer Annie?'
'My dochther Annie she hes walkit oot
Wi' the trumpeter o' Fyvie!'

'Oh hed she been o' high degree
As she's in beauty ready o'
I wid hae taen her by my right hand
Tae make her my ain lady!'

Aul Tifty's tae the castle gaen
Tae lay a charge at Andrew
'My dochther Annie, she is under a spell
O witchcraft wi' Andrew Lammie!'

Lord Fyvie ca'ad his trumpeter,
'Fit's this yiv done tae Annie?
Her faither says ye hae put a spell
O' witchcraft o'er Bonnie Annie?'

'Nae evil airt did I impart
For in this I am canny
But love alane the hert hes won
O' Tifty's Bonnie Annie.'

'Well I must send ye tae Edinburgh toon
For yer safety Andrew Lammie
And ye can't come back for a year or twa'
Tae Tifty's Bonnie Annie.'

Well Andrew sounded his horn shrill
'Yer cattle's lowin Annie!'
'I wid rather hear that cooie low
Than a' the kye in Fyvie!'

'Well I must go tae Ediburgh toon
And for a while I maun leave ye.'
'But, I'll be deid e'er ye come back
My ain dear Andrew Lammie.'

'But I'll buy tae ye yer silken shoon
Tae mak ye o' sae bonnie …'
'Ah, but I'll be deid e'er ye come back
My ain dear Andrew Lammie.'

'But I'll buy tae ye yer bridal goon
Tae mak ye o' sae bonnie …'
'My bridal bed I will belay
In the green kirkyerd o' Fyvie.'

Her faither beat her wondrous sair
Likewise did her mother
Her sisters they did scorn her so
But woe be tae her brother.

Her brother beat her wondrous sair
Wi' cruel strokes and mony
He broke her back o'er the temple stane
O'er the temple stane o' Fyvie.

'Oh carry me doon tae Tifty's steen
And lay ma heid tae Fyvie
That I might see afore I dee
My ain dear Andrew Lammie.'

They carried her doon tae Tifty's steen
And laid her heid tae Fyvie
And it's there she sighed … and it's there she died
But she ne'er saw Andrew Lammie.

Well Andrew hame fae Edinburgh toon
And his hert wis fu o' sorrow
He sounded his horn baith lood and shrill
O'er the green lands o' Fyvie

'Oh Fyvie's lands are lang and wide
And Fyvie's lands are bonnie
But bonnier oot o' Fyvie's lands
Is ma' ain dear Bonnie Annie.'

4

Forests, Rivers and Water

The Key Pool

Some years ago, in a winter blizzard, I stood watching my cousin Helen Mochrie being lowered into the ancient, black kirkyard mools of Tullich. Within the walls is a collection of ancient Pictish stones, raised by Nathalan's pagan ancestors. The pear shape of this walled graveyard reflects the ancient belief that such a shape would prevent the Devil from entering hallowed ground. But with such a powerful saint looking over her bones, my cousin has little need of a wall. As the minister said at the service, 'There is much to give thanks for, having lived a life in the beauty of these hills beside the Dee.' Nathalan himself would surely have agreed. Every Ballater child learns this legend. – S.B.

During the seventh century AD, a boy called Nathalan was born into a Pictish noble family in the land of Tullich near the place known today as Ballater.

He was clever and hardworking, and spent his time helping his tenants grow crops around the fertile banks of the river Dee. Nathalan was a Christian, but he had not entirely cast off the wildness of his pagan ancestors.

In time, a famine ravaged the land, and the poor were brought to starvation by the lack of food. Nathalan immediately opened his granary to feed his countrymen, until all his resources were gone. This helped the people survive the winter, but when spring came, there was no corn left to sow.

His farm lay near the riverbank, where there were banks of soft fine sand. Praying to God, he had the sand scooped up in creels and scattered across the fields. Then, a miracle happened. The sand sank into the ground, where it germinated and grew up as swathes of waving barley and golden oats. It looked to be a heavy harvest.

Then, one sunny autumn morning, all the folk of Tullich went out to gather in this miraculous crop. How horrified they were when a fierce storm brewed in the hills. The Muick and the Gairn poured down from their mountain springs to swell the Dee, which rose in a mighty flash flood to drown the wonderful crop. In an unthinking moment, Nathalan raised his voice to curse God for this act of desolation. Instantly, the flood shrank to a trickle, and all was peaceful again. Guilt took hold of Nathalan; terrible, unremitting guilt. He ordered a blacksmith to forge him an iron chain. This, he bound around his right ankle, and secured to a belt round his waist with an heavy lock and key. He stood before his people and vowed not to return to them until he had travelled to Rome itself to beg forgiveness and do penance for making that dreadful curse. In front of them all, he then locked the chain and tossed the key into the middle of a deep pool in the river, called to this day *Pol-n'-euchrach*, the key pool. Then, he set off alone on the arduous, perilous pilgrimage to Italy.

At the time of Nathalan, the Via Francigena was the main route of pilgrimage to Rome from the North. It was styled the Chemin des Anglois in the Frankish Kingdom, also known as the Chemin Romieux, the road to Rome. It was first mentioned in the third century, and is the oldest of Europe's routes of pilgrimage. After leaving Britain, it winds for 600 miles through Arras, Rheims and Lausanne before arriving at the great city. Catholics who visit Rome or Jerusalem are said to win the right to ask forgiveness from all sins. Traditionally, pilgrims should carry a key for St Peter to Rome. The 2,083km from Britain to Rome would take four long months to walk.

There were many dangers about as Nathalan walked the vineyards, orange groves and pine woods of that ancient road. Natural disasters, disease, local wars and wild animals were all potential hazards, but more commonly pilgrims were ambushed by thieves and murderers for the small amount of money they carried in their purse. Nathalan, to show greater penitence, would have mortified his flesh with cold, thirst and hunger.

At last, he sighted Rome, built on its seven hills. Open fields with views to the Appenines stretched into the distance. The dew was heavy when he rose, amongst hazel groves. His diet was cheese, bread, oranges and olives, and fish where he could get it. The road ran round ploughed fields and narrow dirt tracks. When he reached the Eternal City, he sought out many holy shrines, kneeling before them and praying for God's forgiveness.

After a time, he grew hungry and looked for some cheap food to buy. He met a small boy who sold him a fish for a meager sum. You can imagine Nathalan's bewilderment, when on slitting open the fish, he found the same key inside that he had thrown in the Dee so many months before. Taking this as a sign from God that his sin was forgiven, he unlocked the iron chain that had rubbed his ankle raw on the long hard pilgrimage. The Pope, on hearing of this, was so impressed by Nathalan's piety that he had him consecrated as a bishop. After a time the saint grew homesick for Tullich, and with the Pope's blessing, he made the arduous journey back to the banks of the Dee.

Before he died Nathalan, at his own expense, built three churches, one in Tullich, another at Coull in Cromar and at Bothelin. Until the Reformation, he was held in much esteem; the diseased and sorely-afflicted came as pilgrims to the church in Tullich and returned cured and restored.

At the church he founded north of the Don in Old Meldrum, he saved the villagers from plague by shuffling painfully around the parish boundary on his knees, praying to God to keep the pestilence away.

Donside folk say he is buried at Old Meldrum under a large ash tree, locally known as the Parcock Tree. Nathalan's saint day, 8 January, was held as a holiday in Old Meldrum and in Tullich. Also on the hill by the Parcock Tree, games were held in his honour.

Long ago Cowie, near Stonehaven, was called Collie, and the chapel there was dedicated to St Mary and St Nathalan. In Cowie itself the fishermen recited an old rhyme:

Between the kirk and the kirk ford
There lies St Nathalan's hoard.

Men said that the hoard was concealed in a bull's hide. A rope was tied around the hide, and that rope, according to tradition, would be used to hang whoever succeeded in finding the saint's treasure. In 1541, as in Tullich parish, a fair was established at Cowie by King James V, to be held yearly on St Nathalan's day.

Nathalan's life is described in *The Breviary of Aberdeen*, written mainly by Bishop William Elphinstone. The work was produced using a printing press that Walter Chapman and Andrew Myllar had set up in Edinburgh in 1507. Four copies of the original text are known to exist; one is to be found in Edinburgh University Library, a second in the Library of the Faculty of Advocates, Edinburgh, a third in the private library of the Earl of Strathmore, and a fourth and final edition in the Sir Duncan Rice library of King's College, Aberdeen. But in Deeside, folk need no books to remember their favourite saint.

THE GIANT WITH THE THREE GOLDEN HAIRS, OR, THE SEELY CAP

Of all the tales that Stanley Robertson gave to me, this has always been my favourite. Here is my retelling of it. – G.B.

When Jack was born into the safety of his mother's loving arms, he had no idea of the adventures that lay before him. His weary parents only hoped there would be enough food to fill yet another mouth, for Jack was the twelfth son of a twelfth son, born to a poor woodcutter and his wife.

Unlike the other bairns, this child was born with a seely cap that covered his head. The skin was removed by the midwife and placed reverently into the mother's hands. 'Dinna lose this seely cap,' she said, 'for yer son is born lucky, an' this is a charm that will keep ill awa' fae him.'

Ruling over the land was a cruel and merciless king. Word came to his ear of the child that had been born with good fortune smiling on him. In fact, it was said that the wise woman, the speywife, on seeing the bairn, had pronounced that he would one day marry the king's daughter and sit on his throne. Outraged, the king decided he would go to see this child for himself.

Making his excuses to his courtiers, the king left his castle behind him, and dressed as a rich merchant with cart and horse, he arrived at the forest where the poor family dwelt. He was taken into the crowded home and fed by a tired, thin woman. As he ate of the simple fare, his eyes darted around the room and alighted upon a well-worn cradle in the corner.

'Ye've a lot o' bairns?'

'Aye,' said the mother, with a gentle smile, 'anither een newly born tae!'

'May I see?' asked the man. She nodded, and brought over a warmly-wrapped and sleeping bundle. Her eyes shining, she said, 'This is our youngest son.'

The king made appropriate murmurs of appreciation. 'Another child tae tak care o'. That must be a thocht.' He caught the fleeting shadow of worry that crossed the mother's face and spoke again, silkily. 'You know, I hivnae bairns of ma' own. I wid gladly tak this small lad an' raise him.' The look of horror that crossed the mother's face only made the king more determined.

By the time the woodcutter had reached home, the king had almost persuaded the mother. The two parents anxiously spoke together, but agreed it would be in their son's best interests to be raised by the merchant.

The king left a heartbroken family with a satisfied smile on his face, and in the cart, the crude wooden cradle with a baby snuggled down within, his seely cap hidden beside him.

It was not long before the king found what he was looking for, a deep ravine through which rushed a roaring river. Without a second thought, the cruel man heaved the cradle and its contents over the cliff, and watched as it smashed into the river and disappeared below the surface.

Well pleased with his day's work, the king set off for home. But, had he stayed, he would have seen the cradle re-emerge at the surface, buoyed like a cork, and the child and seely cap, although soaking wet, driven downstream in their makeshift vessel.

Some hours later, a miller was woken by the sound of screaming. Rising, the man made his way down to the millstream. There, swirling in the shallows, was a cradle, and from within came the indignant screams of a wet and hungry bairn. The miller and his wife were a childless couple, and happily welcomed the river child into their home, bringing him up as their very own.

Years later, the king was out hunting, and after a long day, tired and thirsty, he came upon a mill where he was welcomed in and given refreshment by the wife and her handsome son.

'That's a fine boy ye hiv there, madam!' the king said, smiling his thanks as the lad refilled his cup of ale.

'Thank ye, sire,' said the mother, smiling proudly. 'This is Jack, oor lad fae the river.' 'Fit d'ye mean?' asked the king.

'Well, many years ago, a cradle was swept downstream, and we found Jack lying inside! We brought him up as our own!' The king managed to look interested and hide the anger and dismay that seethed in his breast. He looked at Jack and felt hate fill his heart, but his words were warm and friendly. 'Jack, yer a fine lookin lad. How wid ye like tae come an' work for me? Perhaps ye could be a sodger or work in ma palace?'

The king could be very persuasive, and by the time the miller had come home, it was all but decided that Jack would enter the king's service.

'Jack, can ye write?'

'No, sire,' the lad said, his cheeks reddening.

'Dinna worry, son,' the king said genially, 'I'm goin' tae be hunting for a few mair days, so I'll write a letter tae ma queen which ye must tak straight tae her when ye arrive.'

'Yes, yer Majesty,' said Jack, overcome by the sudden change in circumstances and not sure how he felt about them.

Amidst much sadness and promises to return, Jack set off the next day with a satchel of food, the sealed scroll for the queen and his seely cap placed carefully in his jacket pocket. The lad had been given directions, and by nightfall, he guessed he was about halfway to the palace. Rain was falling heavily, and seeing a light from a house, he approached the door and knocked. It was opened cautiously, and a frightened woman squinted out into the darkness.

'Good evenin'. May I come in?'

'No!' she cried, and slammed the door in Jack's face. The rain was driving down, and Jack was soaked, so he knocked again, this time more insistently. Again the door opened. 'Please!' he said, 'I'm soakin'! Jist a warm by yer fire, that's a' I ask!'

The woman looked at the lad, his fair hair plastered to his pale pleading face, and relented. 'On yer ain head be it then!'

She pulled the door wide for him to enter. With great relief, Jack felt the warmth of the fire beckoning, and soon his wet clothes were off and he was wrapped in a rough homespun blanket with the woman clucking over him and plying him with hot soup. Snug, warm and full, Jack lay down on the stone hearth and immediately fell asleep.

Later, the door opened again, and a troop of men entered, all weary, soaked and in a foul mood. They were robbers, and had suffered a bad day. When they saw Jack at the fireside, their first thought was to kill him, but the woman pleaded with them and showed what she had found in Jack's pocket.

'Weel, weel,' said the leader quietly, 'I've nivver seen a seely cap afore! Lads, we must treat this lad wi' respect, an look efter him!'

'An' see fit else wis in his pocket!' said the woman, passing over the sealed scroll to the man. All weariness forgotten, the thief sat down at the table and rubbed his damp hands dry. Then carefully, he unpicked the seal and opened the scroll. He read:

My dear,
When this vagabond hands you this scroll – listen tae this, lads
– please have him executed forthwith.
Your loving husband,
King John.

The robber whistled. 'This lad has made an enemy o' the king! And we all are, are we not, lads?'

'Aye!' the men answered, grinning.

When Jack awoke the next morning, the woman was stoking the fire and there was breakfast laid out for him on the table.

His clothes had been dried and neatly folded, and he checked the pockets to make sure the letter and his seely cap were still in place. After a good meal, he thanked the woman, who smiled at him fondly, and on he went.

He arrived at the palace, and on producing the scroll with the king's seal, he was taken directly to the queen's chambers.

He bowed low and presented the letter to her majesty.

A little confused, the queen opened the scroll, and this is what she read:

My dear,
When this fine lad hands you this scroll, please have him
married to our daughter forthwith. He has proved himself to be
true and worthy of her love.
Your loving husband,
King John.

The queen was not one to disobey her husband, and immediately set about arranging the wedding, which took place the following morning. For Jack and the princess, their marriage was not a burdensome demand, for one look had been enough to know how they felt about each other.

The king arrived home the following day to find himself in the midst of great joy and feasting. On questioning his wife, his face took on a look that chilled the queen's heart, and she knew fear. But as a cloud passes from the sun, the king as quickly recovered, and gallantly welcomed his new son-in-law, despite noting with disgust the look of love between Jack and his daughter.

Later in the evening, when much wine had been drunk and everyone was mellow, the king said mildly, 'Ye ken, Jack, as ma' son-in-law, it wid hiv been customary for ye tae achieve some great feat tae win ma daughter's hand. Wid ye be willing tae please me by doin' this?' Jack did not notice the anxious look that passed between his wife and mother-in-law. 'Of course, sire, anythin' for you!'

'Good, Jack. In that case, I wid like ye tae find the giant wi' the three gowden hairs, an bring those hairs tae me!'

'Where dae I find this giant, sire?'

'Ower hill an moor, through glen an forest, until ye reach the great loch. On an island in that loch is where the giant lives.'

'Very well, yer Majesty,' said Jack, uncertain of his capabilities, 'I will leave at first licht.'

There was a sad parting between the newlyweds as Jack, uncomfortable on horseback, set out on his next adventure.

He travelled far, and by evening came to a village where he found hospitality for the night. However, he was struck by how dour the villagers were, and enquired as to why. 'Och!' said one man, 'this village wis renowned fer its wine! Wine that flowed reid an' rich fae that fountain in the village square. But noo it's dried up, an' we dinna ken why, an' noo we've nae wine an' abody's miserable!'

'Weel,' said Jack stoutly, 'I am journeyin' far tae the giant wi' the three gowden hairs, an' it is said he kens mony things hidden frae man. If I can, I will find oot an' come back an' tell ye!'

The next day he travelled on, and by nightfall arrived at another village, and saw how sad the villagers were here too. One woman told him, 'Fer years we've hid a wonderful aipple tree, an in season it bore gowden fruit, enough tae bring riches an' happiness tae each an' everyone. But these last twa years there's been nae fruit, an' we dinna ken why.'

'Weel,' said Jack, 'I'm awa' tae see the giant wi' the three gowden hairs, and if I can, I'll ask the reason for this an come back an' tell ye.'

Some days later, Jack saw he was nearing a huge silver loch. Far out over the water, he could see an island. There was a small ferryboat waiting at the shore, and in it a disagreeable-looking man, surrounded by a huge accumulation of wealth – coins, gold cups and jewels.

'Good day, sir,' said Jack politely, 'can ye please row me tae the island?'

'Get in, then! An' that'll be ain coin!' said the man grumpily.

Jack paid his fare, stepped into the boat and sat down, looking around at all the riches piled around him. 'May I ask ye a question, sir?'

The ferryman looked up at Jack from beneath his dark and furrowed brow. 'Aye.'

'Why, when ye hiv all this wealth, are ye still a ferryman?'

The man let out a huge sigh. 'Aye, if ye could tell me hoo tae leave this life, lad, I wid gladly gie ye a' these riches. This is an enchanted boat, an' I am trapped rowin' it, for I dinna ken hoo tae brak the spell!'

'Dearie me,' said Jack, shaking his head. 'Weel, I'm awa' tae see the giant wi' the three gowden hairs, an' if I can, I'll find oot an' tell ye on ma return.'

'If ye return,' said the man moodily. 'Mony dae not, ye ken!'

Jack was silent for the rest of the journey, wondering what fate awaited him.

From the shore, it did not take Jack long to reach the giant's huge, dark castle. When he rapped on the heavy oak door, the sound echoed cavernously within. The door opened slowly, and there, to his surprise, was a small woman. 'Oh!' said Jack, 'good day!'

'Fit are ye doin here, lad?' said the woman worriedly.

'The king has sent me tae get three gowden hairs frae the giant who bides here.'

The woman looked horrified. 'The king sent ye tae yer death, ye mean!' Then, with surprising strength, she grabbed Jack's coat and hauled him in through the door.

'Hiv ye any idea o' the danger yer in, laddie?' she barked as she dragged Jack through to the kitchen.

'I'm beginning to ...' he said meekly. At the fear in his voice, the woman looked at him, and her angry expression softened. 'Yer jist a bairn, look at ye!'

With that, she sat him down, and Jack told her his story, of his seely cap and his journey, marrying the king's daughter, and how he had come to be at the giant's castle. When he had finished, the woman looked at Jack. 'Well, I think I'll jist hiv tae help ye, lad.

Noo the giant will be returnin soon, an' ye must hide, or else he'll hae ye fer supper!'

It was a few minutes later that there was a huge wrenching of the door and a voice roared, 'WUMMAN! FAR'S MA SUPPER?'

Thundering footsteps deafened Jack as the giant trudged through to the kitchen. The woman rushed around, speaking soothingly to the huge ogre. Jack could hear sounds of food being placed before the giant, and then slurps and crunchings as he ploughed his way through six oxen.

Replete at last, the giant belched an almighty belch. 'Now, wumman, croon me tae sleep!' The giant lay down on the ground, his huge ugly head heavy in the little woman's lap. At once, she began singing softly, and very quickly, Jack could hear the sound of snoring ... then, 'OWWW! FIT DID YE DEE THAT FORRR?' The woman had pulled out one of the giant's golden hairs!

'Oh, sorry, ma' dear, it wis a fly. I thocht it wid wak ye, so I tried tae slap it awa',' she said, as she stuffed the golden hair into her apron pocket. 'Noo yer a wee bit wakened, could ye tell me somethin that's bin puzzlin me?'

'Fit?' asked the giant gruffly.

'The village that his a wine fountain, fit why does the wine nae langer flow?'

'There's a toad underneath the fountain. If they dig it oot, the wine will flow again ... noo let me ... sleep ...'

Soon snores could be heard again, followed by another huge yelp from the giant. 'WUMMAN!' he roared, 'FIT ARE YE DEEIN!?'

'Oh, I'm so sorry, ma' dear. It wis a spider that time!' She placed the second golden hair in her pocket. 'But as yer wakened, can ye please tell me why the villagers wi' the gowden aipple tree nae langer hae ony fruit?' 'There's a rat gnawin at the roots! If they remove it, the tree will bear fruit again ... noo ... let me sleep ...'

For the third time, the sound of snoring filled the kitchen, only to be followed by an earth-quaking screech! 'AGAIN!!?'

'Oh, ma' dear, that wis a nasty ant that time. It wis jist awa' tae bite ye!' She tucked the third hair away. 'But as yer wakened, ye ken the ferryman?'

'AYE!'

'How can he leave his boat?'

'A' he must dee is haund ower the oars tae anither, an' he will be free … noo, YE MAUN LET ME SLEEP!' The woman hurriedly began to stroke the ogre's face once more, singing softly until his loud snores drowned out her voice.

Very carefully, she took the three golden hairs from her pocket and handed them to Jack, who had slipped out from his hiding place. With a mouthed 'thank you' and a grin, he turned and made his way quietly from the castle.

When Jack reached the ferryman, the man looked up at him in amazement, and hope was in his eyes. 'Ye made it, lad! Well? Did he tell ye the answer?'

'Tak me tae the far shore an' I promise tae tell ye,' said Jack.

When he hopped out of the boat onto the sand, Jack turned to the man. 'The next man that seeks the ferry, gie him the oars, an' the enchantment will be broken, an' you will be free tae gang far ye please!'

The ferryman's eyes filled with tears of gratitude. 'Och, lad, I dinna ken hoo tae thank ye, but noo ye maun tak a' these riches. I'm sick tae the death o' them!'

When Jack arrived back at the castle, he was leading his horse, for he had bought a cart to contain all the riches he had been given. Not only had the ferryman insisted on giving him all he had, but the villagers whose apple tree now flourished had gratefully laden him with golden fruit. From the other village, he had been gifted with many bottles of the richest red wine. The princess, the queen, and the courtiers at the palace were overjoyed to see Jack return, but the king was not.

Jack presented his father-in-law with the three hairs, but he was not interested in them, and cast them aside. Instead he looked with jealousy on the riches Jack now possessed.

'Where did you take all this from?' he growled.

'These treasures were given tae me, yer Majesty, an' thanks tae you and the giant wi' the gowden hairs, I hiv made mony freens on the road!'

The next day, the queen discovered that the king had gone. He had decided to journey to seek riches for himself, with help from the giant on the island. His envy of Jack gnawed at him, and his greed for possessions consumed him.

He passed through the villages where Jack had been so welcomed, but his bitter gaze was seeking riches, and he found none in the smiles and kindness people showed.

When the king eventually reached the great loch, he found the ferryman waiting in his empty boat, a smile on his face. Approaching, he snarled, 'You there, I am yer king. Ye'll row me over to the island richt noo!'

'Yes, yer Majesty, of course,' said the ferryman merrily. 'If ye can jist hop into the boat an' hold the oars fer jist a wee moment …'

At the palace, the queen, the princess and Jack waited in vain for the king to return. When it appeared that he had gone for good, there was no great mourning in the castle, but rather the joyful coronation of a new king and queen.

The couple had wonderful children of their own, and Jack's parents were brought to stay at the palace. And so it was that Jack and his queen lived contented, and ruled wisely for the rest of their days.

Riddle Six
I will never leave, but remain
Always changing, but still the same.

THE WIZARD LAIRD OF SKENE (1665–1724)

I am an old woman now, but when I was a child, my grandmother used to tell me stories about the Wizard Laird of Skene. When she was a young girl, she married a farmer, Matthew Booth, and in 1906 came as his bride to his farm at Hillhead of Carnie, Skene. You can imagine her surprise when on Halloween she saw bonfires being lit in fields around her. This, she later told me, was to ward off the Wizard Laird of Skene whose very name struck fear into folk long after he was dead.

I myself have spoken to farmers in Dunecht who recounted his exploits as if they happened only yesterday, and were quite convinced of the warlock's powers.

You may say that this is fancy, superstitious nonsense. But Stanley Robertson, a former gypsy traveler who visited this area, has been quoted as saying:

> If there is something demonic about a place, the frisson will rise up your back instead of down. That is why the hackles rise at the back of your head. And that is exactly the feeling I got when I once visited Skene House – my hackles rose and I had the feeling something very evil had taken place there.

In the queer way that the world turns, for ten years of my marriage, the wizard was one of my closest neighbours, buried in the lair of Skene in the quiet little hamlet of Kirkton of Skene, just over the dyke from our cottage. Local children claimed that if they ran a hundred times round the wizard laird's gravestone, he would rise from the dead, but none were ever bold enough to try it. The author William Somerset Maugham heard the wizard's story while recovering from tuberculosis at Glen o' Dee Hospital in Banchory, Kincardineshire, and used it as inspiration for his novel The Magician. *– S.B.*

What manner of folk were the Skene family? The Skene arms bears three daggers with wolves' heads. Robert, the first Laird of Skene, was granted the Barony of Skene by Robert the Bruce in 1317. It is said that he was a powerful hunter, skilled with the *sgian* or dagger. King Robert was in the area chasing deer when his horse reared as a massive wolf stepped into the path before it. The king was flung to the ground and the great beast was like to tear his throat out, when his namesake leapt to his rescue and plunged his dagger into the wolf's black heart. There and then the king awarded him the name of Robert of Skene, and created him baron of all the lands around that a hawk could cross in its flight.

The seat of the family was Skene Castle, later called Skene House, near the village of Lyne of Skene. It had a dark forbidding loch within its grounds, a suitable nursery for such a formidable warlock. Its walls were 10ft thick; its central tower built in 1217. When Alexander Skene was a young man, local folk say he travelled to Padua in Italy, where the Devil himself presided over a school teaching the Black Arts to any interested followers. Skene progressed well in his studies of necromancy and astrology, staying there for seven years. Men say that the Devil wanted to keep his best pupil with him and trod on his shadow to stop him leaving, but Skene used a dagger to cut his shadow off, and so escaped. Ever after, he was said to be 'the man without a shadow'.

When he eventually returned home, he gathered around him four weird familiars; a crow, a raven, a magpie and a jackdaw, which chattered and flew around his head as he ventured deep into the woods at night in search of poisonous ferns and noxious herbs for his magical preparations and experiments. The jackdaw in particular was said to possess powers almost equal to those of its master.

Skene was not a man to be trifled with. On one occasion he paid for a night's stay at a roadside inn, where a ceilidh was in full swing. The wizard ate his meal in grim humour, for he was solitary by nature and not over fond of loud music, badly played. Wearying of the *stramash*, he transported himself back to Skene House, but not before putting a curse on all the dancers and musicians. The musicians were condemned to play till their fingers bled, and the dancers were unable to stop dancing until their feet, too, bled copiously. The ceilidh eventually ended when everyone present collapsed with exhaustion.

He had the power to 'reest' a man to the ground, by simply staring at him, until the ploy ceased to amuse him and the person was free to move again. But his greatest achievement, without a doubt, came one Halloween, and a very frosty one at that. He told his coachman, Kilgour, to have his coach and two black horses ready and harnessed outside his house at midnight. He further warned him that he would have a visitor with him, and that on no account was Kilgour to turn round to look at the 'guest', or it would go ill with him.

As ordered, the coachman drew up outside Skene House at midnight, the horses' breath rising cloudy in the frosty air. He did not dare turn round when the wizard and his guest took their seats behind him, and he followed the order to drive for the Loch of Skene 2 miles to the south.

It was a bitterly frosty night, as extracts of the old poem by A. Gordon of Cluny tell us:

> There liv'd in the north in the days of yore
> A laird deep skilled in magic lore
> In ae nicht's frost, by an oath he swore
> He would drive o'er the Loch of Skene.
>
> On locks an' snecks fowks fingers stuck
> If they outside should crawl
> An' they who shivered in the neuk wad cry
> 'Preserve, it's caul.'
>
> His hair stood up and his knees did knock
> When the laird ahint him to someone spoke
> And was answered again by a raven's croak
> Which shook a' the Loch of Skene.

On reaching the black waters of the loch, covered only by a thin sheet of ice, Kilgour made to reign in the horses, but the wizard would have none of it, and ordered him to whip them forward. Terrified, the coachman half-turned to look down at the figure behind him. To his horror, the feet protruding from under the cloak of the wizard's guest were cloven, those of the Devil himself. With that, the ice cracked, instantly pitching the wizard's two black hounds, which had followed, into the eerie water, where they drowned. But on the far bank awaiting the coach was a coven of local witches, who grabbed the reigns and pulled the coach to safety.

Every frosty night since then, if you're bold enough to go and see for yourself, you can see the ghostly wheel tracks made that night rise up to the surface, and you can clearly discern where the back wheels skidded on the far shore. No fish ever swims; no bird ever flies over that eerie track.

Powerful though he was, the wizard was still mortal, and the time came when he was very close to death. It was a cold, dreich autumn evening. From the sulphurous pit of Hell, the Devil had arrived, ready to collect the soul of his favourite pupil, but the wizard had one last trick up his sleeve. The Devil having a weakness for gambling, he managed to get His Imperial Blackness to agree to settle his fate on the outcome of a fight to the death between two of his familiars. The birds were to meet on a large flat stone within sight of the house, where Skene lay on his deathbed. The agreement was that if the magpie won, the wizard would have a Christian burial and his soul would be pardoned and set free. However, if the raven won the contest, the Devil would claim him, hair, head and heart.

Tradition says that the birds fought for over two hours, bloodied and ripped in feather and claw, but with a huge effort of will, the magpie gathered the strength to rip the raven apart. The wizard died at peace, and was laid to rest in the kirkyard. Some say his coach and horses were buried with him, and that heavy chains were originally hung around the grave to keep him down, but there's no current evidence for that. The last of the family line was another Alexander, born deaf, dumb, and nearly blind. He died in 1827, unmarried, childless, and some say, unfairly cursed by the wicked deeds of his ancestor.

But the loch is still there, and the strange, hideous, wrought iron dragons and gargoyles decorating the mighty policy gates.

And down by the loch side, the ruins of a small folly, a Greek temple stands, as if waiting for some ancient god to enter. Through the dripping thorns and weeping willows peer stone statues of storks and fierce wild boars, and always, wherever you go, a raven watches, its eyes two orbs of evil.

The Pedlar

This song has been a favourite of mine since I first heard Stanley sing it once on Bennachie. I was delighted to hear a ballad that appears to have travelled far through time, yet retains much of what we associate with Robin Hood and his merry men.

Stanley used to emphasise the mystery surrounding the pedlar. He was obviously wealthy and trained with a bow, so extremely strong, but in the song he never discloses his true name. It was dangerous to do so; a name was never disclosed to anyone without good cause, as it was believed this gave a person power over you. – G.B.

A pedlar brisk and a pedlar thrawn
And a pedlar cam loupin o'er yon lea
When wha should he meet but twa troublesome men
Twa troublesome men they chanced for tae be.

'What's in yer pack noo, ma stoot fellar?
What's in yer pack noo? Come tell tae me!'
'I hiv seven shirts o' the finest silk
Besides ma bow strings two or three.'

'Well upon my word,' cried Little John
'Half o' that pack it belongs tae me!'
'But there's ne'er a man in a Scotland
Can tak ma pack awa' frae me!'

Then Little John picked a broad, broad stick
And the pedlar did the same

And they both did fight, and they both struck blows
Till he cried, 'Noble pedlar, haud yer hand!'

Then up spake bold Robin Hood
He was sittin ahint on yonder tree
'Well, I'm a better man than thee
And I shall tak that pack frae thee!'

Then Robin picked a bold, bold brand
And the pedlar did the same
And they both struck blows, and they both drew blood
Till he cried, 'Noble pedlar, haud yer hand!'

'And since yer a better man than I
Perhaps yer name ye'll tell tae me?'
'It lies a' tween ma' ain breistbane
Whether I tell ma name or nane.'

'But ma name it is "Stoot Feller"
I wis pitten oot frae across the sea
For the killin o' a man on ma Faither's land
Tae the greenwood I wis forced tae flee.'

The Reel o' Tullich

When I first began writing, I knew nothing about outlets, reviews, distribution and publication. My father immediately suggested that I 'contact the laird', as the lairds on Deeside are always seen as protectors of the arts and culture in the region, from the Games to local plays. I duly wrote to Lady Farquharson of Invercauld, who was very supportive, although my first novella, a romantic fiction about the Black Colonel (fortunately) went unpublished (it was Mills and Boon in a kilt). So my view of the Black Colonel is not that of the Clan Gordon … – S.B.

Highland dancing is thought to date back to the eleventh century. Some say it was invented by a young man who went to hunt a deer. So gracefully did it leap that he couldn't muster the will to kill it. 'Why have you brought back no venison?' his hungry family asked. In reply, he held his hands up like the stag's antlers, and showed them how beautifully the animal moved.

The old kings of Scotland traditionally used Highland dancing to test how strong and able their men were for war. The Gordon Highlanders of the North-East used Highland dancing to keep their soldiers battle-ready (in a six-step Highland fling, a dancer will jump 192 times). The regiments could dance up to twenty steps in one dance. At first, only men were allowed to perform these dances, but during the world wars of the twentieth century, women began dancing to preserve their culture and history. Today, 95 per cent of all dancers are female. The costume worn by girls today is called the 'Aboyne dress', named for the Aboyne Highland Games, where only boys may wear the kilt. Sometimes the girls' dress is called a 'Flora MacDonald' outfit, with its light, flared tartan skirt and petticoat and laced up bodice.

The Highland fling was said to have originated in the hunting seat of King Kenneth McAlpine at Braemar to celebrate the defeat of an enemy in battle. It was performed on a targe, a circular shield of wood covered in deerskin hide. The front of the shield was festooned with brass studs and plates. There was a long spike in the centre, which the performer would dance around.

The sword dance is referred to in documents dating from the reign of Malcolm III, King of Scots, in the eleventh century. He is said to have danced over his bloody claymore crossed with the sword of his defeated. Thereafter, the sword dance was performed on the eve of battle. It was believed that if the dancer touched the sword with his foot, he would be wounded, but if he kicked the sword, he would be killed. Today, if a dancer touches a sword he loses five marks, but if he displaces the sword, he is disqualified.

The *Seann Truibhas* is Gaelic for 'old trousers', and was developed after the 1745 Jacobite Rebellion when kilts, plaids, pipes and weapons were outlawed. In 1782, this ban was lifted, and the dance shows the Highlander kicking off the hated trews.

The Reel of Tullich, a group dance, had stranger beginnings, and needs a little background information. The Farquharsons are one of the main clans on Deeside, with branches at Braemar, Monaltrie, Finzean, and Inverey. The chief of the Inverey Farquharsons was the Black Colonel, Iain Dubh Farquharson of Glen Ey. He is famed as a warrior, a Gaelic poet, and ladies' man. He was said to be very handsome and very loyal to his Tullich tenants. What else could be said of such a chief? Today he haunts the Pass of Ballater, or so my father told me when I was a wee girl, and there are those who have seen his ghost ride his great black horse up the cliffsides of the Crag of the Falcon, as he did once when escaping the Redcoats. Once, when fleeing from the Redcoats, Iain Dubh cleared 18ft at every bound, escaping over a boiling mountain river with another gigantic leap. The spot now has a bridge, named Drochaid-an-Leum, the bridge of the leap.

What manner of henchmen had Iain Dubh? McDougall was the fiercest, fiercer than all the wolves along the Dee put together. Men said when he gathered firewood; he would haul a whole birk tree up by the roots with one pull, and drag it home as light as a girl's ribbon. The Black Colonel summoned McDougall by firing a shot from his pistol at a target that hung on the wall. They would practice fighting till McDougall snatched up the colonel's terrier and threatened to break its jaws.

The colonel's mistress was Anna Bhuidh Bhan, who stayed at a small cottage at Ruigh an t-Seilich. His wife and family on the other hand, resided at Balmoral. The colonel divided his time between the two. If the Redcoats were particularly persistent in dogging him, he hid with Anna at 'the Colonel's Bed', a cave that is partially concealed by the river Ey. When Anna eventually died, her people buried her in the kirkyard at Inverey. Iain Dubh, the Colonel, wrote a lament for his lost love, for he was a great Gaelic poet as well as a fine warrior.

Marjory Leith, his wife, heard it sung everywhere she went. Furious, she summoned McDougall, and asked him to write a parody of it, with the promise of a keg of the finest whisky when he'd composed it. Soon, it was written and McDougall went around the countryside singing it:

> Ochadan's shiubhal Anna
> Dh'fhag sid mise car tamuil fo bhron
> A chaoidh cha teid ise as m'aire,
> Qua am faigh mi im agas aran eorna.

Which translates as:

> Alas! You are gone, Anna
> Leaving me in deep sorrow
> But never shall your memory eave me
> Until I get butter and bere bread

Unfortunately for him, the colonel heard it. Immediately he ordered that all the stocks of butter and bere bread in the glen be brought to him, along with McDougall. McDougall was made to sit at the top of the table directly opposite the colonel, who pointed two loaded pistols at his head. Iain Dubh then indicated a huge plate laden with bere bread and butter, cocked his pistols and ordered his prisoner to eat. The wretched man ate till he was sick and fit to burst, before the colonel relented and kicked him out.

But to return to the business of the reel. In the little clachan of Tullich was an inn called The Stile o' Tullich, and the small kirk of St Nathalan. Deeside winters are beautiful but fierce, and one horrendously snowy Sunday, the Black Colonel had to struggle hard to navigate through the snowdrifts from Glen Ey to the kirk of Tullich. When the laird arrived, the cold had worsened and the snow had developed into a blizzard. The minister who was to perform the Sunday service had even further to travel. The congregation in the kirk were by now frozen stiff.

Iain Dubh felt sorry for his tenants. 'Let's roll a keg of whisky from across the road from the inn to the kirk!' he suggested.

No one needed a second bidding. The keg was duly rolled into the kirk and the bung drawn. Soon, communion cups were produced and filled with drams. Then, a fiddler went up the little street and came back with his fiddle. The dancing started, and at its height they invented a new dance, and they called it the 'Reel o' Tullich', to the cheers and applause of their laird.

The kirk rafters rang with hoochs and skirls, laughter and ribaldry. Then a soutar climbed into the pulpit, and two weavers and three tailors pretended to be elders. A few courting couples were led in jest to the 'cutty stool'. The blacksmith, a great burly Highlander with a full beard, stood up in the precentor's desk and sang:

John come kiss me noo
John come kiss me noo
John come kiss me by and by
And mak nae mair adoo.

After this, two couples went outside and slithered up to the rooftop of the kirk, which was up to the eaves in snow, and danced on the snow-laden thatch, singing:

Ower the kirk an ower the kirk
An ower the kirk tae Ballater!

But in the middle of this spontaneous ceilidh, who should arrive but the minister. Outraged at what he saw as sacrilege, he cursed each and every dancer. Of eighteen pairs of Ritchies who danced that day, all were dead within the year. Remarkably, the colonel was still very much alive; proof, some said, that he was indeed 'sib tae the Deil.'

When eventually the colonel did die, it was in the depths of winter. His burial was as eventful as his life had been. On his deathbed he requested that his body was to be laid beside his mistress, Anna Bhan, at Inverey. His sons overruled this plea and buried him instead in the traditional chieftain's lair at Castletown in Braemar.

Next day his coffin had risen to the surface of the ground, through 6ft of hard-packed ice and snow. His sons reinterred him. This pattern was followed for a fortnight, with the colonel's ghost growing increasingly angry and aggressive, with nightly visitations to his sons.

Finally, he wore them down so much they ordered his coffin to be exhumed. Deep drifts made it impossible for horses to transfer him up the Dee, and so the coffin was placed on a sledge and dragged to the river. There it was placed on a raft and towed upstream to Inverey, where at last he was reunited with Anna Bhan, his sweetheart.

Two Farquharson clansmen stepped forward to pull the ropes away, but the colonel's eldest son, Peter, intervened to stop them.

'Leave them alone,' he said, nervously. 'My father might want to rise again!'

Peter was nothing like his father, being peace-loving and mild-mannered. When his clansmen grew rough with drink, he would mutter:

Se mhuinntir sibh. Se mhuinntir sibh, agus 'sann agaibh bha mhathair mhath, a dh'ionnsuich sibh.

Which translates, it is said, as 'You are a sad lot, but then you had a good teacher.'

Riddle Seven
A bottomless pit
To put flesh and blood in

AULD CREUVIE

Some of my most precious memories with Stanley Robertson are from the drover's road up at Lumphanan, a favoured haunt for travellers. Stanley showed me the camping ground and the midden, where broken crockery, old reins and holey buckets were thrown.

On the road itself, some old, old oak trees bend their leafy limbs across the path, and there, Stanley, with great respect, used to shake hands with Creuvie and ask to pass peacefully.

One day, a group of us travelled up the old road. The weather was foul, and although not well, Stanley asked us to act out this story. I can still see his tall, arresting figure, black in the rain, his voice ringing out while we traipsed around in the mud acting out being trees, wizards, heroes and heroines! – G.B.

On a green hill up from Lumphanan, there stood a ring of sturdy oak trees that looked down over the little glen below. Scattered over the hill were sheep, gleaming white in the summer sunshine, with their herder Jack prone in the leafy shade of the oaks, savouring the cool breeze that gently wafted through.

Jack was a fine young man who worked hard for little pay, though he was always cheery. He worked for the laird, a mean man, who everyone knew dabbled in the Dark Arts and had never a good word to say to anybody.

Throughout the day, and especially at night, Jack was out on the pasture, thwarting would-be sheep stealers and protecting against predators. And so, most days, Jack's mother would climb up to where the sheep were grazing with food for her son.

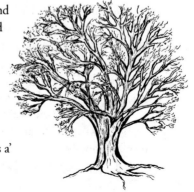

'Thank you Mither. I've a right hunger on me … and there's cheese the day!' grinned Jack.

'Aye, a' wis at the market yesterday and a' sold a' the jumpers a' made! So a bocht us a wee treat!'

'That's braw, Mither, and the sheep's wool is comin oot in han'fu's jist noo, so look, I hiv anither sack tae ye.'

Jack's mother smiled wearily. The laird had no thought for his tenants. She lived in a very rundown cottage, and had still to find the rent. Without the wool to weave into clothing to sell, she would have been very much worse off.

'Any news for me the day, son?' she asked, lifting her face to the sun.

'Weel,' said the lad, finishing off a mouthful of bread, 'the birds seem tae be fair excited. I've been noticing they seem affa restless.' Even as Jack spoke, a cloud of birds flew up into the sky, chattering noisily.

It was two days later, Jack had been enjoying a snooze in the shade of the mightiest oak tree on the hill when he was woken by the birds in the branches above. Jack loved to be outdoors. He knew every bird, tree and flower, and felt free beneath the big skies that were so often the roof over his head. He was very much one with nature. He could understand the creatures, and they could understand him.

So when the birds began to twitter and call out to one another, Jack spoke out to them. 'Birds! Are ye weel? Ye seem sae restless and unsettled! I thocht at this time o' year ye'd be sae busy feedin yer young ye widnae hiv room fer chatter!'

A thrush flew down to the grass beside Jack. 'Laddie, this is a special day. It is Midsummer, and something will take place on this hillside that only happens once every fifty years!'

'Tell me!' said Jack. 'Fit is it?'

'Auld Creuvie, the King of the Trees, and the other oaks, will uproot themselves to dance in the magic of the night. They will move downhill to court the young, slender trees at the bottom of the hill. All the birds are leaving before tonight, for who knows what strong magic will bring?'

'That soonds amazin',' said Jack blissfully.

'But it will not be safe for you to be here, Jack!' insisted the thrush anxiously.

'Oh, dinna worry. I will tak care o' masel!' he replied.

Later that morning, Jack made his way to the laird's castle. As he approached the gates, he came upon the laird himself, who looked up suspiciously. 'Aye, Jack. Fit is it?'

'Good mornin' tae ye, laird. The birds are affa chittery the day!'

'I ken it weel. The sky's been derk wi' them!' he complained.

'Weel, a wee bird telt me the nicht's a special nicht, fan a' the oak trees will uproot themsels tae gang an' dance wi' the young trees at the bottom o' the hill.'

The laird's eyes widened, as if he had just hit on something considerable, and he gave Jack a dark look. 'I dinna want the herd on the hill the nicht! Awa' somewye else!'

'Aye, sir, I winna pit them in danger.'

'An bide awa' yersel!' he spat angrily.

Jack nodded to the laird, touched his hand to his cap, and turned to go back to the sheep.

The kitchen maid was out beating carpets, the dust swirling round and forming streamers in the light. She stopped for a moment to sneeze, and saw Jack. She smiled, and he grinned back. 'Good mornin', Jean! An' bless ye!'

Jean laughed, her already rosy cheeks blushing. 'Mornin', Jack. It's fine tae see ye. awa' back tae yer sheep?'

'Aye, I wis jist telling the laird aboot the trees on the hill …' and Jack began to explain to Jean what the night would bring.

'… an' I'd better nae dawdle ony langer, fir the laird's watchin'! Tak care, Jean.'

'Och, awa' then, but come back soon!'

Jack grinned again, and walked on with a lighter heart. He was very fond of the lass, and one day he hoped he would have silver enough put by to ask for her hand.

The thought of Jean made the hike back up the hill a quick one, but he was hot and thirsty by the time he got there. He was fair delighted to see his mother toiling up the hill with a pail, and was even more pleased to find a bottle of milk and some bannocks inside.

But his mother was looking anxious. 'Jack?'

'Aye?'

'Ye ken that it's Midsummer's Day?'

'Aye, an did ye ken aboot the trees, Mither?'

'I jist minded on it last nicht! The last time it happened wis so lang afore, I wisnae affa big.'

'Weel, tell me!' said Jack, his eyes dancing.

'Ma Mither telt me that a' the big oak trees pulled themsels oot o' their restin places, an' made their wye doon the hill tae dance fir a whilie. But in the holies left ahint, there were a kinds o' riches – jewels an' sich like!' Jack's eyes grew large. 'Aye,' his mother said, nodding, 'I thocht that micht surprise ye!'

'Can I tak ony jewels, Mither?'

'Aye, ye can, but jist a couple o' things. Dinna be too greedy.'

Jack nodded, smiling. 'Mither, this could be sich a help tae us!'

'I ken, lad, but ye hiv tae tak care, it's verra strong magic. Look, I've made ye something.' From her apron, she took out a piece of knitting. Curious, Jack unfolded it. It was a line with loop handles in place at regular intervals all the way up. He thanked his mother, and stuffed it in his pocket.

'Noo I ken ye will be there the nicht, but promise me ye'll tak care.'

'I will, Mither.' He pulled her little frame close. 'Dinna worry yersel'.'

She smiled up at him bravely. 'I'll see ye soon! Noo, I must awa', I hiv mair knittin tae dae!'

It was not long after his mother left that Jack heard a sound like a rising wind. He looked up into the sky as an endless stream of birds rose up out of the oakwood, into the blue, flying westward. The air seemed so still when they had all gone. The afternoon passed slowly, the only sound the rustling of the oak leaves in the breeze. Jack led his flock through a gate to an area where they would be safe from the dancing trees but he could still keep an eye on them.

As evening approached, the sun descended, and Jack heard a stirring in the oaks that brought his neck hairs to alert. He had been sitting on the grass beside the trees, but now he made his way up the hill, and lay down where he was concealed by some great bleached stones.

A thrumming had begun, and to Jack's sensitive ears, it sounded to him as if the trees were singing. It sent a thrill to the core of his being, and although the breeze had diminished, the lad watched as the great oaks began to sway back and forth.

The light was almost gone from the sky when Jack saw a dark figure flit up the hill. It was the laird.

The laird scurried up the hill, intent on finding the greatest of oaks, Auld Creuvie's resting place. With a triumphant yell, he dived into the largest of the pits. Jack settled for the hole nearest to him, and peered down. In the gloaming, a hoard of treasure gleamed brightly, and grinning, Jack jumped in, searching for small but valuable treasures to take back with him. A bonny bracelet of pearls caught his eye – he immediately thought of his mother – and there, a ring with a stone. That would look grand on Jean's hand.

Well satisfied, the young man placed the treasures in his pocket, and made to leave the pit. But to his horror, he discovered the floor had sunk, even as he had taken the treasures. His mind moved quickly, figuring how he was to get out. The night was blackening, and the sides of the pit were sheer.

'Jack? Are ye there?'

'Jean? Is that you?' The relief in Jack's voice rang out clearly.

'Aye, but I cannae see ye!'

Jack then had occasion to remember his mother's gift. 'Jean, I'm awa' tae throw ye a rope. Look out an' catch!' Jack threw the wool as far as he could, and Jean snatched it as it appeared out of the darkness.

'Did ye get it, lass?'

'Aye, I'll throw an end doon tae ye!'

Before long, Jack had hoisted himself out of the hole and, calling to Jean, rushed over to where he had seen the laird disappear. The largest hole yawned deep and dark.

'Laird, can ye hear me?' Jack strained his ears, and from a great depth he heard a wicked chuckle. 'Laird! Cam awa' noo, it's nae safe! The mair ye tak, the further ye'll sink!' he shouted, as loudly as he dared. But there was no reply. The riches the laird had found had consumed him. He was greedily filling his sacks with no other thought in his mind. Nothing would sway him.

The pair called and called till their throats were raw, becoming more desperate as the musical thrumming of the trees once more began to fill the air. The great oaks were returning to their resting places, but the laird did not care.

In the twilight, Jack and Jean retreated back up the hill and watched as the dark shapes of the oaks swayed and swaggered grandly back to where they came from. Magic filled their senses, but it gradually began to lessen to a murmur, a whisper, and then, silence.

The laird was never seen again, and so his nephew inherited the estate. He was a considerate gentleman, and saw to it that all his tenants were comfortable, ensuring that homes were in good condition, and that his labourers were paid a worthy wage.

This change of circumstances greatly pleased Jack and his mother. It was not long before Jack was able to propose to his dear Jean and present to her a lovely ring with which to seal their promises to one another. Well contented, the little family lived and worked near Lumphanan for the rest of their days, but their memory of that Midsummer's night was never forgotten.

The Kelpie Tale

In many places around Scotland, the legend of the water kelpie is told. Often this magical creature would take the form of a beautiful and docile horse, enticing the unsuspecting victim to ride on its back. Once in the saddle, the kelpie would plunge back into the river, taking its rider with it, never to be seen again. – G.B.

Jake walked out of the alehouse, hauling his packs along the cobbled road. He had such a long journey ahead of him. The weather was hot, and as he stepped onto the bridge, he was glad of the cool breeze stirred up by the river. He rested his arms on the sun-warmed stone. The ale, bread and cheese were still there in his belly. Deep, dark water flowed beneath the bridge, forming swirls that twisted the reflections of the green trees overhead. It was very peaceful.

There were salmon fishers resting down on the riverbank. They were mending their nets, but everyone and everything seemed lazy in the summer sun. One fisherman looked up and nodded to Jake, who lifted his arm in greeting and then sighed; the packs at his feet were solidly awaiting his attention. With a groan, he hoisted one after the other onto his protesting shoulders, and turned to walk over the cobbled bridge, his head bent with the weight. Immediately, the dull ache in his back returned.

A whicker caught his attention, and he straightened slightly. Before him was a chestnut horse with a white flash and large, warm brown eyes. It carried a halter and saddle, but was not roped to the rings that lined the brig. When it saw Jake looking at him, the creature trotted towards him, its mane swinging, and gave a gentle whinny.

'Ye bonny beast,' said Jake quietly. 'Far's yer maister?' The horse came closer, and this time lowered its head. Jake could never resist animals. He smiled, crooning, and once more lowered his packs to the ground. He fumbled in his pockets, frowning, and then his face cleared. 'I thocht as much! Here's an aipple tae ye, ma beauty.' The horse stepped up to Jake and delicately nibbled the fruit from the flat of his hand while Jake stroked its nose.

'Weel? Who d'ye belang tae?' At that, the horse looked at Jake, then bent its head and gently nuzzled his arm. 'Me?' said Jake laughing. 'Ye want tae be mine?' The horse raised its head, gently whickered once more and turned so its saddle was facing Jake. Then it stood, waiting patiently. Jake looked at the horse, and then glanced back towards the alehouse and over the bridge, but there was no one else in sight. 'Weel … I suppose …' The horse turned its brown eyes on Jake once more. He shrugged. 'I canna look a gift horse in the moo!' he said laughing, and bent down to heave his packs onto the horse's back, tying them on expertly.

He took hold of the saddle, placed one foot in the stirrup, and was about to haul himself up when he heard a cry of alarm. 'NO!'

From the other side of the bridge, a red-faced man came puffing, his arms flailing wildly above his head. 'Get doon!'

Before Jake had time to react, the horse beneath him suddenly screamed, and rose up on its hind legs, its eyes rolling madly in its head. Jake, one foot stuck in the stirrups, was thrown backwards and sideways, and was in great danger of being struck by the beast's flying hooves. It screeched and thrashed, and Jake was thrown free, his foot released. The nightmare creature turned, rearing up once more in order to stamp and crush the helpless man under its vicious hooves. More yells and pounding footsteps came from across the bridge. The monster seemed to leap into the air, over the stonework, and a great splash was heard as it plunged underwater.

It was as if the world had been holding its breath. The trees stirred, light seeped through the branches, and the birds, which had been silent, began to chirp once more. Jake, dazed, but only bruised and shaken, turned to see his red-faced saviour bent over him, trying to catch his breath. 'Nae a horse,' the salmon fisher gasped, 'a … kelpie!'

It was then that Jake began to shake as he realized how close he had come to his end. And what of the loss of the packs? It was a small price to pay for his life. From that day onwards, Jake was watchful of both horses and watery places, but decided it was always better to walk.

5

COAST AND SEA

SMUGGLERS OF COLLIESTON

For years, the village of Collieston and others close by thrived on the fishing trade. It was renowned for Collieston Speldings – salted, sun-dried haddock and whiting, which, being of delicate flavour, were popular in Edinburgh and even London. In the late eighteenth century, during the summer, the village children left school to dig bait and collect mussels for the line-fishing on which the locals depended.

Fifty years later, with the arrival of bigger boats and drift nets, the fishermen could no longer sustain themselves and, having a harbour that could only accommodate small fishing vessels, many moved away from Collieston to the bigger towns.

In the sixteenth century, the Earl of Errol was a staunch Roman Catholic who lived at the old Slains Castle, and owned all the land around Collieston. In 1594, following the Earl's betrayal, King James VI ordered his castle to be obliterated by cannon. He had plotted to overthrow the king with the aid of the Spanish, which might explain the wreck of a galleon that lay for many years further up the coast. The ruined tower of the castle can still be seen on the cliffs north of the village.

During the Reformation and the reign of King James, religious fervour was high, and many in Collieston were condemned and burned or hanged as witches. Despite the 'cleansing', Collieston remained firmly Roman Catholic, but it appears that after the Jacobite rebellion, the community was absorbed into the Church of Scotland.

But old loyalties run deep, and as taxes rose, especially the excise duty on spirits, so did the activities of the smuggling trade, or 'Free Trading' as it was known. It had always been a part of village life, but now it became vital to survival. Gin was a popular trade item, involving many in the local community, and some of the more respectable ministers! Collector Allardyce of Aberdeen Customs described Collieston as 'the principal haunt of the smugglers for landing goods', and the inhabitants as 'a turbulent riotous pilfering set'. The rugged coastline around the village was particularly suited to smuggling. – G.B.

Although every villager knew the signals for when a ship was offshore and ready to offload its illicit goods, it was left to a few to know the hiding place of the contraband. Philip Kennedy was such a man. He was a farmer up at The Ward, along with his brother John.

The coastline is strewn with little inlets and coves, some with sandy beaches, others with caves, many of which are only accessible by boat. Kennedy knew the land better than any other man, and he had laid out his plan to only a few. They then relayed censored information to the rest of the villagers.

'Right, William, awa' ye go, an' you too, James – there's the ship's signal.' The two boatmen rowed out from the sandy beach at

Cransdale. The night was perfect, with little wind, plenty rain and most importantly, a sky with no moon.

'It's derk as hell, Philip!' whispered John nervously, shivering in the bitter cold.

'Aye,' said Philip, rubbing his frozen hands together, listening for any sound that might indicate the gaugers had been alerted.

Depending on the size of the haul, every villager knew the drill. Sacking would be tied to their horses' hooves and wrapped around the bridles to minimise sound. Cartwheels would be muffled, for all knew exactly the risk they ran.

Philip, John and the two rowers had been out for most of the day. It was December, and the weather had been murky and dreich. The daylight had never really breached the clouds – ideal for the smugglers. It had taken nearly all day to dig out the deep pit on the beach. The sand had been laid out on two canvas sails – the upper sand on one, the damp lower sand on the other. When the goods arrived, the sand would carefully be replaced, so that if the hiding place was examined, there would be no change in the colour of the sand – from light to dark – in a dug-out spadeful, indicating no disturbance and averting suspicion. Its depth had been determined with great care, for it had to be deeper than 6ft, which was the length of an exciseman's searching spear. It was then lined with wood to prevent collapse. It was an exact labour, but in Philip's mind it was business, and he was well practised.

The brothers' ears strained to hear the sound of the rowers' return. As soon as the pull of the oars was heard, a signal was sent up the cliffside for the villagers to come down to help transfer the goods – sixteen ankers of Dutch gin – into the already prepared pit, one anker being the equivalent of ten gallons.

Everything went as planned, with the villagers working like a well-oiled machine. The pit was only to be a temporary hiding place.

The following night, the four men returned, along with servants from the farm. Once again, it was murky and dark as sin. The plan was to transport the goods up the cliff onto waiting carts, then to take the spirits and hide them on the farm in a location only known to the four. From there, the haul would be distributed overland to various locations.

It was another laborious task, digging up the barrels.

'I canna see a thing!' complained John.

'Good! That means we canna be seen deein' fit we're deein', ye daftie!' Philip muttered derisively, his words obscured by the rain.

'A've hit a barrel, Philip!' puffed James. 'Ga' canny noo!'

Before long, the goods were being loaded up onto backs and creels, the men straining up the steep and slippery path to where hushed figures were waiting with the carts to carry the gin to the farm. Silently, the line of men and horses plodded along the track, the only sounds the rain and the squelch of feet and hooves in the mud.

'Halt!' shouted a voice, and the smugglers were suddenly blinded by the light of uncovered torches. There was a panicked scrabbling as men vanished into the night, but not Philip and his brother John. Brandishing sticks weighted with lead, they advanced towards the gaugers and began to flail at them fiercely.

'Draw yer swords, men!' yelled a voice, and at once, the sound of ringing steel could be heard. In the rain and flickering torchlight, John was heard to scream as a cutlass found its mark.

Fearlessly, Philip waded in and cracked his stick over two of the men, felling them with blows, and then restraining them.

'Enough, ye scoundrel! Let ma men go!'

'I winna! awa' wi' ye, or it'll be worse for them!'

The gauger left John where he lay, unconscious in the rain and mud, and lifting his cutlass, he cut down on Philip's head before the smuggler had a chance to defend himself. The stroke cleaved his head open. Philip slumped to the ground, his lifeblood pouring from the wound. John lay still where he had fallen. There was no sign of any of the other men or servants, for they had all deserted.

The gaugers scrambled around and grabbed the horses, carts and creels. Afraid of reprisals from other villagers, they disappeared into the village as quickly as they could drag the horses.

In the dark, the two men were left bleeding in the mud, the track silent but for the drizzle of the falling rain.

Some time later, Philip moved, and gradually he regained consciousness. Eventually, he staggered to his feet, and with blood still pouring from his head, he managed to make his way to the nearest farmhouse, Kirkton of Slains.

Philip knocked heavily on the door and almost fell inwards when it was opened.

'Kennedy, man! Yer blooded!' The farmer caught Philip as once more he fell onto the flagstones unconscious.

The farmer and his wife lifted the dead weight of the man as blood continued to pour onto the floor, and laid him on a settle. They tried to stay the wound, but Philip had lost too much blood and his whole body was pale to death.

Towards morning, he stirred, and his eyes opened to see the anxious faces of his carers looking down at him. A bitter smile flitted across his ashen face.

'If a' had bin as true as me, the prize wid've bin safe and I widna' be bleedin tae death.'

As a watery dawn lightened the dark sky, he breathed his last. Philip Kennedy was deeply mourned by his brother, who survived, and the rest of the village. But some of the community could not raise their heads for the shame of deserting this brave, unyielding man.

❧

That December was not the only success of the excisemen. Triumph on the water was also achieved.

The Dutch ship, the *Crooked Mary*, had been the courier of the contraband gin that fateful night, creeping inshore to Cransdale in the dead of night. She came as close as she dared, signalling to the waiting smugglers as to which inlet she was making for.

As soon as the goods had been transferred, the ship flew back out into deep waters where no ship could arrest her. The crew, buoyed with success, weighed anchor, and all enjoyed a nip of rum as they discussed plans for their next delivery to Peterhead.

Little did the ship's crew know that Captain Ayre, skipper of the King's cutter, was tracking the *Crooked Mary*, as he had tried unsuccessfully to do many times before, but this time he smelt success.

The first indication the crew had of their arrest was a roar as Captain Ayre and his men leapt aboard. Unprepared, the men submitted meekly to the boarding.

'We are outwith the limits, mister!' smiled the captain of the *Crooked Mary*. 'You will never prove otherwise!'

Captain Ayre grimaced. 'Oh, I'll prove ye were! An up tae nae good the nicht!'

The High Court heard the case, and as Ayre could not look to the villagers of Collieston for witnesses, he went inland to New Deer to try and find proof of the ship's guilt …

'Aye, yer Honour! A keekit oot ma back door an' I saw the lugger close tae land! An' there wis Captain Ayre's cutter cam intae arrest it!'

'And how could this be, Mr Mitchell, fan it wis a filthy dark nicht wi' nae moon, and yer hoose is ten miles inland an yer back door looks inland?'

'And ye say ye saw the *Crooked Mary*, madam?'

'Weel … a' think a' did, sir … it wis derk, an' I wis staundin on the beach.'

'Beach, ye say?'

'Aye,' the woman said bravely, avoiding the judge's eye.

'Madam, there isnae a beach there. It's a steep cliff.' There was silence from the witness. 'Mrs Collie, hiv ye ever been tae Collieston?'

'Em … actually … I nivver hiv.'

Despite the fact that Captain Ayre appeared to lack any credible witnesses, the High Court recognised the risk of allowing the

Crooked Mary off the hook, and decided for the sake of Crown and Country to relieve the Dutch captain of his ship. The lugger was given over to a gleeful Captain Ayre.

Ayre waited until the excitement had calmed down, and then sold the ship back to its previous owner for a tidy profit of thirty pounds.

It is to be wondered, where, if anywhere, an honest person can be found?

Riddle Eight
As dark as night
Fringed by colour
Flooded by light
I give sight

THE CURSE OF FORVIE

Many years ago, there was a village on the coast of North-East Scotland known as Forvie. There had been a settlement on this land since the Stone Age, and today, remnants of flint and arrowheads occasionally emerge from the sand that now covers the buildings. Only the kirk itself remains, and of that, only a wall.

The story of how the village was buried has been lost, though legend has it that this area was cursed. In my research, I came across a manuscript that shed some light on this tale.

There have always been those excited by history, and in 1832, Lewis Smith was one who was keen to find traces of the past. He decided to go to the auld kirk of Forvie with a companion to see if there were any relics to be had.

As they dug, only the odd piece of rusted metal appeared. They were just about to give up when the other man hit something and uncovered a flat stone, which Smith rightly presumed was a lid covering a small urn. Within, he found a number of things, including a well-preserved manuscript.

The title of this parchment was 'Ane true and veritable historie of the awful visitation by quhilk this hail parish of Forvye, with the exceptioun of the churche and minister's hous was buryed undernethe vast hills of sande. Indyte't by the Minister, anno, 14-.' – G.B.

In the fifteenth century, Sir Malcolm Cheyne was the laird of Forvie, and so resided in the castle.

The local minister had noticed that although Malcolm Cheyne had provided the monies to build and equip the kirk of Forvie, and had ensured that the Abbot of Deer provided a pastor for the church, the laird himself had then made a point of having nothing to do with it. Whenever the minister met the laird in passing, he did not find him a likable character, but rather a deceptive man, filled with avarice.

So he was surprised when one day he received a summons to come quickly to the castle. 'Fit ails yer maister?' asked the minister to the servant who had brought the message. 'He's taken affa poorly, sir. Near tae death, we think!' answered the man.

'Dearie me! Weel, let's hurry alang!'

The minister was ushered into Laird Cheyne's chambers. The man looked dreadfully sick, but the pastor saw that it was not just a physical ailment, but that the man was tormented in spirit. Quietly, he sat down and smiled gently into the troubled eyes of the gaunt-looking man.

'Laird, I'm here fer ye.' A momentary look of relief passed over the laird's face. 'Aye, minister, thank ye for comin.'

'How are ye, sir?'

'Nae sae good, as you can weel see. But it's nae just ma body, it's ma mind, minister, ma mind! I've relied on riches a' my life, an' noo I'm faced wi' unimaginable terrors!'

'There is yet hope …'

'Even fer crimes sich as mine?' Cheyne asked desperately.

'I ken not yer wrongdoin, sir, but I see hoo ye hiv provided the parish wi' a church.'

'Dinna think I did that fer ony religious reason! Mony years ago, I wis very ill. I felt the angel o' death hovering ower me, an' I wis looking desperately fer a wye to assuage ma guilt fer all ma wrongfully acquired wealth an evil deeds. So in the midst o' ma torment, I promised a church fer the parish, an' I began tae recover. In ma invalid state, I fulfilled ma vow, but as ma strength improved, I began tae despise an' mock ma decision, an' would have revoked it, but it wis too late. I wholeheartedly turned ma back on that weak time an' fully embraced ma auld evil life once mair.'

The minister could see how it had exhausted the laird to speak for so long. 'Yer no alone in this, sir. Mony o' us only turn tae God in oor times o' anguish and distress. I trust that noo ye believe, yer turning from yer evil ways is genuine.'

The exhausted laird appeared uncertain and harassed in mind.

The minister carried on. 'If ye want tae ken forgiveness an' peace, the best thing ye can dae is tae share the dark burden yer carryin.'

'If I hae breath, an' ye will hear me, that is fit I intend tae dae, minister.'

The man paused as if gathering strength, and then he began. 'When ma faither passed oan, he left maist o' his estate tae ma elder brither, Alexander, leavin me wi' a paltry sum that wid barely keep me fae starvation. I felt deeply insulted, an' resolved tae tak revenge by takin fit I rightfully believed wis ma share! Outwardly, I wis the biddable brither who supported Alexander, an' did everythin I could tae mak masel' indispensible tae him. He wis duped and entrusted me wi' his finances, an ensured that I wis given a princely sum fer ma efforts!

'Little did he ken in his joy o' spendin that I wisnae watchin ower his fortune, but instead helpin him tae squander it, for ma only desire wis tae reduce him tae a pauper. An I wis well on the wye tae doin so when he becam sick an' I saw anither opportunity … I poisoned him, an' he died.'

The pastor shuddered involuntarily. It was harrowing to hear, and watch the agony that this wretched man was in.

'But that isnae the worst o' ma crimes,' whispered Cheyne. 'What I did tae his lovely dochter wis infinitely worse. Her mither hed died sometime afore, an' I couldnae leave her tae become heir, so I callit up a favour fae some wicked pirates that I hed befriended an' offered tae pay them tae mak her vanish tae a foreign shore.'

The man's face crumpled in his distress. 'I can still hear her cries an' pleadins fer mercy. They hiv tormented me through the years! The men nivver returned, and I hed tae presume a' were lost at sea, so I made recompense tae each freen or family affected.'

The minister was horrified, but kept his face calm.

The sick man was silent for a time, his weary face lined and drawn with bitterness and pain. He closed his eyes, and the minister thought he had drifted into a tormented sleep. But the eyelids flickered, and he groaned, and then said, 'So, whaur wis I? Oh aye, a murderin uncle …'

He smiled without humour and continued. 'So … I inherited a' ma brither's estate an wealth, an' fer the last thirty years, I hiv lived as a king, and continued wi' mony wicked an' evil deeds. But noo I wish tae mak recompense.'

His eyes pleaded with the minister. He lifted a weak, fleshless hand and pointed to a letter on a table. 'I hiv written doon that if ever ma niece should return tae Forvie, the hale o' the estate belangs tae her. But in the event that she nivver returns, I wish a' ma worldly goods tae be dedicated tae the church …'

The minister was glad to be able to bring relief to the burdened, dying man, and on Cheyne's death, he carried out his wishes.

But it was not the minister's fault that a servant had been listening in on the conversation that had taken place in the laird's chamber. It was only natural that such choice information should be shared with others, and it went round the small community like wildfire.

The minister was very concerned that in Laird Cheyne's will there had been no provision made for his three daughters, and so he had gone immediately to visit the Abbot to seek his wisdom and advice. It had been agreed that there would be a stipend given by the church to ensure that the young women were provided for, and housed adequately, if not quite in the manner to which they were accustomed.

Imagine the minister's horror on returning to discover that the village had risen up as one, and had taken revenge on the evil laird. They had none to lash out on but his offspring. There is no telling now if the lassies had followed their father's evil ways, but the villagers descended on these vulnerable young women, tied them up and flung them into a boat, which was not caulked securely, and set it on the tide, shouting cruel and hateful obscenities as only heated blood can invent.

In their distress and hate and disbelief at this awful reverse of their circumstances, the women screamed for mercy, and seeing none was forthcoming, their panic turned to curses:

Yf evyr maidenis malysone
Dyd licht upon drie lande
Let nocht bee funde in Furvye's glebes
Bot thystl, bente and sande.

Their boat miraculously did reach dry land, and as soon as its keel was hauled up to safety, a storm broke out. It was a dreadful storm of wind and rain that lasted for nine days. When it eventually blew itself out, there was nothing left of Forvie but the manse and the church. All else was buried deep beneath the sand and has remained so to this very day.

If you visit Forvie, you will find a most beautiful nature reserve where curlews call over lonely moors and gulls ride on the breeze. Many rare flowers grow here in abundance, and all around are wonders to be seen. But beneath all that are buried the lives and memories of those who, on that dreadful day, sought to judge the lives of three young women for their father's evils.

In the saugh of the wind, their pleading voices can sometimes be heard.

THE KNOCK MAITLAND STANE

The following song was inspired by the Book of St Fittick.

I visited the wonderful exhibition at the Maritime Museum on 'The Cheerful Vale' which gave detailed information on findings at Tullos and Torry.

In the seventeenth century, Aberdeen Harbour was not navigable by bigger ships because some areas of the riverbed were too shallow. Dredgers managed to largely solve this problem, but one stone evaded their skill, and proved too stubborn to remove. David Anderson, known locally as Davie-do-a'thing, was the man who devised the solution. Below is the song I wrote, inspired by this intriguing tale, set to the tune of 'Wee Wullie Winkie'. – G.B.

In the harbour moo,
There wis a muckle stane
Richt in the wye o' boats
It proved tae be a pain!
But fan they tried tae shift it,
It widna budge at a
It obstinately stuck in the grun,
Like a limpit tae the wa!
Fowks shook their heids
An scratched their beards an a'
They christened the stane,
'Knock Maitland'
An they gied a sigh or twa
But years did pass an naethin wis deen,
Naebidy hed a clue!
Till a chiel ca'd 'Davie-do-a'thing' said:

'I'll dee it nae bither noo!'
At the ebbin tide
Fan Knock Maitland wis exposed
A heap o' barrels Davie brocht
An tied them on wi' force
Fan a wis secured wi' rope,
He placed hissel upon its pate
For the flowin tide this canny chiel
Did sit an' smile an' wait!
The watter swirl'd roon
An' the barrels did gently sway
An' Davie's muckle grin grew mair,
As he felt the rock give wye
Whit a roar cam frae the shore
As Knock Maitland it did glide
An' floated Davie-do-a'thing awa' –
Noo the harbour wis bonny an' wide!

The Lass from the Sea

All over Scotland, tales are told of the seal folk, the selkies. Here is one that will be familiar to many. This happening took place on the banks of the Don before there was a road bridge, at a time when selkies and mermaids were not the stuff of legend, but were known and seen, bringing wonder in their wake. – G.B.

Many years ago, there lived a fisherman named Angus, a lonely man who bode in a hovel on the banks of the Don. Each day, he would net fish in the estuary. Some he would keep, but most he would sell.

One night, Angus could not sleep. Hearing unusual sounds from the small island on the river, he quietly made his way down to the water's edge, hiding amongst the rushes and the willow that grew there. The moon was bright and illuminated the scene before him.

On the island, he could see a ring of lassies dancing, their naked skin shining in the moonlight, and strange wild music filled the air. Angus gazed in wonder, entranced. With his heart racing, he silently made his way along the riverbank, over the Brig, and down the other side.

The girls were occupied dancing, and they did not see the dark figure wade through the shallow water and creep to the sand spit. Here the lassies had discarded their skins, for these were selkies, the seal people, enjoying the glow of the full moon in which to dance the night away.

Angus carefully edged onto the wet sand and snatched one of the skins. Just as quietly, he slipped back the way he had come, and arriving home, he carefully stowed the skin in the eaves of his hut.

As dawn began to lighten the sky, the selkies one by one resumed their true form as they dressed once more in their own skins, then each returned to the water. Except for one. She darted about, unable to find her skin, her cries calling her sisters back to the surface of the water, though none could help her. As the sun rose high in the sky, the distraught lass lay down and wept as if her heart would break.

It was then that Angus called from his hut across the water. The girl looked up in panic, afraid of any human contact, but this man's voice was gentle and reassuring. A blanket in hand, he made his way across to the lass, all the while murmuring kindly to this terrified creature of the sea. He wrapped the blanket about the selkie's shivering form and led her back to his hut.

Soon the cot-town heard that Angus had taken a wife. It was not long before there was one child, and then another and another, filling the little dwelling to the brim.

And what of the selkie lass? She never forgot where she came from. Each night, whether the water was still or rough, she would sit at the river's edge, crooning her wild seal songs, and mourning the loss of her life at sea.

Angus adored her, and the children grew up wild, dark-haired, and wonderful swimmers. The lass, although unusual, was known and loved by the locals, for she could cook the most wonderful seafood, and decorated the home with shells and other trinkets from the seabed.

Late in the evening, her sisters would sometimes come and sing to her from the safety of the water, but none dared to return to their human form, lest they too be trapped on land.

Some years later, on a beautiful late autumn morning, Angus took his wife aside. Fish were becoming scarce, and he would have to take a berth on another man's boat and travel far to catch enough to feed his growing family. He assured his wife and children that he would return in a few weeks, and he said his sad farewells.

Time passed, and the winter cold began to set in. The two older children, fine strapping lads, were set to repair the thatching on the inside of the leaky roof, when one let out a shout. He came down the ladder awkwardly, carrying something heavy and wrapped up in oilcloth. The family crowded round as he untied the bundle on the floor.

When the mother saw what was within, she let out a gasp and a wail, and sank to the ground. For there, as fresh and wet as the day she had lost it, was her own sealskin. She stroked it, then held it to her, breathing the familiar scent of salt and sea, and she wept. At first, they were tears of joy, but as the realisation of her husband's deception and betrayal dawned, her weeping became uncontrolled, mingling with screams of rage at being robbed of her life for so long.

The children could not console her, and they cried too, unable to comprehend their mother's grief. When finally she could weep no more, she laid her precious skin down, tucking her feet into its familiar folds, determined never to let it out of her sight ever again.

Taking her children in her arms, she quietly told them her story once more. It was familiar to them, but as the youngsters listened round-eyed to the tale of how she had come from the sea, the truth began to dawn in their minds. They thought this tale had been just a bedtime story, but now a fear began to grip at their young hearts, for they could hear the hunger and yearning in their mother's voice.

The youngest held her tightly, and each of the children pleaded with their mother not to leave, but nothing would dissuade her. She embraced them, and gave her reassurance that she would return, that she would not forget them, but the children felt the finality of the parting.

Down by the river's edge, the selkie once more dressed herself in her skin. As lithe as seals can be, she darted smoothly under the water, only to reappear at the surface a moment later, her head sleek and dark in the cold, bright sunlight. Despite the screams and howls of her children on the bank, she dived once more into the depths of the river and did not come up again.

When Angus returned the following week, his hut was no longer the home he had left. The bitter sadness of the family's loss tainted all their lives, and nothing could quell their loneliness.

Every morning, when the children went down to the water for a sight of their mother, they would always find three silver fish left on the riverbank for the family. And whenever the children swam in the river, the shadow of a seal would join them in their sport, and for a time they would know the joy of their mother's presence.

But never again did they see their mother in her human form.

POWER FAE BEYOND THE GRAVE

Stanley loved tales of the supernatural, and it was he who told me the story of the 'keeper of the graveyard'. Legend has it that the last person to die in a graveyard is its keeper, and as such has power over any living being that enters the cemetery. As soon as another dies, the evil

influence is broken. The following tale took place by Portlethen village
many years ago. – G.B.

Alec was a well-known face around the villages. He was often to
be seen mending a dry-stane dyke, repairing a roof or helping out
on a farm. This autumn, work had been slow, and although Alec
never usually approached the big house, he decided to try his luck.
He knew one of the manservants well; he was the brother of the
blacksmith in the village.

It was Hugh who answered his knock. He was not looking his
usual cheery self.

'Good mornin', Hugh!'

'Aye, Alec.'

'Ye look like ye've seen a ghost, man!' laughed Alec, trying to get
a smile from the clearly distraught man. He was pale and sweating,
and though he attempted a smile, Hugh was obviously in no mood
for playful conversation.

'What brings ye here, Alec?'

'I wis jist wonderin if there's ony work tae be had aroon' the
hoose?'

A strange look came over Hugh's face, one which Alec could not
define. A blanching? Relief?

'What's up wi' ye man?'

'There's been a death.' He indicated for Alec to come in. 'I'll tell
ye aboot it ower a dram.'

The kitchen was empty when they entered. There was none
of the usual cheerful bustle that you would expect first thing in
the morning. Curious, Alec sat on a stool by the fire and took the
proffered dram. Hugh sat down opposite him and took a swig
from his own cup. He wiped his mouth, and looked over at Alec as
if weighing things up.

'There wis a visitor cam tae the hoose a week ago. He met the
laird some months back fan he wis doon sooth. Onywye, ae day
he cam tae the door uninvited, an' the laird couldnae dae less than
offer him hospitality.' Hugh put down his cup on the flagstoned
floor. His hands were shaking. He clasped them together.

When he looked back at Alec, the hairs on his neck rose. Although not an easily frightened man, he felt a shiver of apprehension.

'Fit?'

'An evil man,' whispered Hugh. 'From the time he entered this hoose, it wis as if a shadow hed crossed the threshold.' He swallowed. 'Bad things began tae happen. The master becam affa poorly, there wis strange sounds an' smells a ower. The man hung dead creatures up aroon' the hoose … an' caul … it wis affa caul in the rooms an' corridors. It wis as if this man,' he spat out the word, 'hed stirred up a' the evil he could.'

'Why did he come?' asked Alec, intrigued, despite his growing fear.

'Apparently Black Jo, as we ca'd him, wis seekin somethin for his magical purposes in this hoose, an' threatened the laird wi affa consequences if he didna allow it.'

'So fit's happened?'

Hugh swallowed. 'Last nicht, we heard groans an' screams o' obscene laughter comin fae his chambers. It woke abody. Then there wis a huge sound like … like … an earthquake!' Hugh's eyes stared wildly. 'We a' felt his passin'.' He shivered. 'It was as if a hell hed been let loose … an' then … he wis gone.'

'Gone?'

'Aye, he died.' Hugh sighed, and covered his face with his hands. 'None of us hiv dared to gang up tae his chambers this mornin.' He was silent, then looked up. 'Alec, wid ye go?'

'Me?' Alec looked horrified. Hugh's face shone pale. 'Please?'

Alec went over in his mind what Hugh had said. How bad could a dead body look? He looked up resolutely. 'Aright, nae bother.' He swallowed nervously. 'Show me far tae go.'

Hugh's face relaxed slightly. 'Thank you, Alec. The maister will pay you weel.'

Hugh led Alec up the servants' stair. Their footsteps echoed in the silence. Alec felt nothing untoward, but his heart was hammering against his ribs as they came along the carpeted corridor to the chamber. Hugh silently stood back, and Alec stepped forward, his mouth dry. He felt lightheaded. His hand shook as he reached for the door handle. He turned it, and the door swung in easily.

It was the smell that hit him first. He coughed and couked, and with his hand covered his mouth and nose. The room was glaringly bright, the curtains carelessly flung wide open, and it took a moment for his eyes to adjust. But then it took all of his strength of will to remain there. He clutched the door for support, his eyes wide with fear. The body of Black Jo lay contorted on the floor, his face turned upwards with a look of horror and rage etched into the lines round his gaping mouth and eyes.

Alec swallowed, his head taking control, though the urge was to run, to be out in the green, golden morning, away from this dreadful horror.

'Hugh, come awa' in. We need tae get this cratur washed, and intae a windin sheet,' he said hoarsely. Hugh edged round the door, and stood rooted to the spot.

'Hugh!' said Alec sharply, and felt a flood of relief that here was another as scared as himself.

Hugh started, his eyes very black in his white face. 'Aye, I'll get watter.'

Two hours later, the body was washed, wrapped in a sheet and placed on the bed. It had been not been easy to straighten the twisted limbs, but it had somehow helped the two men to get on with the task in hand.

The room was tidy; assortments of unmentionable things, dark, dead and rank had been thrown into a pail and covered, to be burned later. The windows were wide open and the stench of death was fading, when there were footsteps outside in the corridor. The two men jumped. It had been so quiet.

The youngest servant, Susan, peered round the door, but her scared face softened, as she saw nothing untoward in the room.

'Hugh, the laird is up and well again!' she said, with relief in her voice.

'Oh Susan, that is good news!' smiled Hugh, the colour returning to his face. 'Well, hopefully that's the last o' the evil fae this gent!'

He wiped his brow. 'Breakfast time, Alec, a' think! Susan, can ye run an' tell abody we're a'most done here, an' for cook tae mak us a fine meal?'

'Aye!' she said, grinning, and went off running.

Two days later, the body was buried. There had been some debate as to whether it warranted being laid to rest in the hallowed ground of a graveyard. There was no service, just a roughshod casket, which was placed in the earth as hurriedly as possible. The grave was left unmarked.

Alec was paid well for his services, and soon was regaling the local village with tales of the nightmare. He had treated himself to a proper bed at the inn, and had made himself very comfortable.

On this, his second night, he was woken by a strange whisper. Suddenly, he was wide awake. A voice was calling his name as if from a great distance. Horror clutched at his heart. What was this? Quickly, he dressed and crept quietly out of the building. The night was black as he followed the voice. He moved through a black wood, his feet reluctantly moving towards the source of the call. The moon was rising as he found himself before the graveyard.

'Alec! Alec!' cried out an eerie voice from within. It sounded distressed. Before he could stop himself, Alec had stepped through the gate, and instantly was gripped by something unearthly, from beyond the grave. He felt himself being engulfed, but although he struggled, it was in vain and moments later, his body slumped onto the dew-soaked ground.

Towards dawn, Alec rose, shook his head, and made his way from the graveyard. He did not seem to notice his damp clothes, his deliberate footsteps, and that every now and then a hiss would escape his leering lips.

When the man came in sight of the big house, he began to trot, then run, and a whisper escaped his lips.

'It is MINE! No-one else may have it!'

The front door was easily unlocked, and with the agility of a cat, he was through it in an instant. He moved purposefully up the stairs, not making for the chamber of Black Jo, but instead towards the servant quarters, to Susan's small room. He flung open the door. The startled lass sat up in bed, her face convoluted in horror as she saw a huge figure lunge towards her. Before she could scream, a clammy hand was clasped over her mouth.

The smell of death pervaded the chamber, and from the man's mouth came a whisper. 'Give the stone to ME!'

Susan stared at the face above her in terror, then her eyes rolled back in her head and she fainted. The man threw the lass back down on the bed and he began to rake around the room, but could not find what he was looking for. He turned to see Susan stirring, and in his rage took her by the throat.

'Give it BACK!' he screeched. At that moment, he stopped, his great hands releasing their hold from round the petrified servant's neck, and the body of the man slumped down to the floor.

About a week later, Hugh and Alec were sharing a farewell dram by the fire in the kitchen.

'I'd never heard on that before,' said Alec quietly. 'The keeper o' the grave, you say? He hed power tae call me an' tak ower ma body tae do as he wanted?'

'Aye,' nodded Hugh. 'Puir Susan, I hope she'll recover.' He looked sober for a moment.

'Aye,' said Alec sadly. 'I'd nae pairt in what happened that nicht. It wis as if I wis a puppet on a string and there wis naethin I could dee.'

'It's just as weel aul Maggie died at that moment, and became the keeper o' the grave herself, an' Black Jo lost a his power, otherwise ye'd hiv been deen for murder!'

'I ken,' said Alec soberly. 'D'ye ken fit it wis efter?'

'Susan foond this bonnie reed stone lyin under Black Jo's bed fan she wis cleanin the chamber efter the funeral. She popped it in her apron, meanin tae show the maister. Ma guess is that's fit that ghoul wis efter, an' probably wis fit he'd been searchin for a' the time he was here. The maister said it was fae the hilt o' a sword, the origins o' which are a bitty dark … so he threw it in the river!'

'Good riddance,' said Alec quietly.

'Thank you, Alec, for your help,' said Hugh. 'It's been quite a nightmare.'

'Aye, I'm nae sure I'll be back this wye in a hurry,' Alec smiled.

And he never was.

6

THE CITY

THE STORY OF BENHOLM'S LODGINGS

So many years have passed since this beautiful old building was first erected. From the Tillydrone Avenue entrance into Seaton Park, this turreted dwelling house rises gracefully before the eyes, its rough stone walls and deeply recessed windows recalling a time long past.

In one recess still stands the knight; sadly, his sword is long gone, but his faithful dog still sits with him. Unappreciated, this unique building stands with its windows boarded up, a sad air of neglect about it.

There is word of a reprieve; local residents are eager to see it open to the public, and are looking to secure funding for renovation and fill it with bustle once more. Many think the site for Benholm's Lodgings is incongruous, but after examining the history, I find it oddly appropriate. – G.B.

George and Robert's father was William Keith, the Master of Marischal. Their childhood days were spent at Dunnottar Castle. As young boys, the brothers had spent many a day venturing up and down the cliffs. Robert was the fearless one, plunging into all kinds of mischief with his wooden sword in hand. George, however, the cautious one, always thought through the best, most secure strategy and executed his plans with precision. Robert's schemes usually ended in disaster, punishment and disgrace. So, even at a young age, a divide began to grow between the brothers.

In the castle, George was always the favoured one. Robert – rash, hotheaded and impatient – was a lovable rogue, and he was the locals' favourite until his early teens, when his pranks developed into serious situations where young women were often involved.

George, on the other hand, began to take his position as eldest son very seriously indeed, knowing that heavy responsibilities lay ahead of him, and he purposefully began to distance himself from his brother. There was general relief when Robert left home to turn to soldiering.

In 1581, the 4th Earl Marischal, William Keith, died and George, at the age of twenty-eight, succeeded his grandfather as the 5th Earl Marischal, a position held by the Keiths since the time of Malcolm IV and William I.

George was made for his role, and rose to every challenge to become a trusted advisor to King James VI. In 1589, he was sent to Denmark as the king's ambassador to broker the marriage between James and Queen Anne of Denmark.

George was perhaps best known for the founding of Marischal College in 1593. His vision was for a more outwardly focused university than King's College. In 1609, he was appointed Lord High Commissioner to the Parliament of Scotland. He was a man of prestige who invoked confidence in all whom he met and worked alongside … except, perhaps, his brother.

Robert had become a fearless soldier, and had learned some lessons from the rashness of his youth. He and his brother crossed paths many times, despite their very different lifestyles. Robert worked with his brother to see Peterhead founded as a town in 1587, after the king granted it a burgh of barony, and a charter, which permitted a harbour to be built.

Robert watched his brother's fame and fortune grow. His wealth and influence seemed to know no bounds and, naturally, as the younger brother, this grated with Robert. For him, this was untenable. He could no longer stand being the poor relative, and sought to redress the balance, yet he had learned not to rush into situations, so he spent time planning how best he could gain from his brother's abundance.

Earl Marischal George Keith was of course a very rich and influential man. He and others had benefitted from the turbulence of the Reformation, where lands, especially those belonging to the church, had been seized and passed on to families in the king's favour. The Keiths were one such family.

George's uncle, Robert Keith, was the Commendator of Deer, and in 1587 was designated Lord Altrie, a peerage granted by the king. George and Robert Keith between them – and at the behest of the king – owned large swathes of Scottish lands.

The younger Robert's masterplan was ready to be implemented. In 1590, he captured and garrisoned the lands of Deer Abbey, which were owned by his rich relatives. He was aided by a band of supporters, who may have been offered reward, or perhaps followed Robert out of devotion.

Indignant, both George and his uncle gathered a force of men, including forty armed citizens of Aberdeen, and advanced on the Abbey. On seeing that retreat was necessary, Robert headed west and took refuge in Fedderate Castle, hauling up the drawbridge, thus securing him and his men in a strong position. The surrounding terrain was flat and boggy, and from the castle's towers, Robert's force could fire upon any advance party that sought to attack.

It was a stalemate for George and Lord Altrie. Disgusted, they eventually had to offer Robert sweeteners to back down. Whether he received lands or his knighthood is not clear, but Robert relinquished his hold on New Deer. However, he was obviously not quite satisfied with the arrangement, for in 1593, both brother and uncle made an official complaint to the Privy Council that Robert had taken unlawful possession of the Earl's house, Ackergill, in Caithness.

The result of this was Altrie's signation of the lands and barony of Benholm in the Mearns over to Robert in 1594. In addition, he now held lands in and around Aberdeen, including Seaton, which had previously been the Bishop's Ward, and also gained properties in Upperkirkgate and Netherkirkgate.

Around 1612, the now knighted Sir Robert, satisfied as a man of means, had his own residence built in Aberdeen, in what would have been a beautiful country setting, just outwith the burgh boundary. He made his 'toun hoose' a defensible building with two round towers, reinforced with thick walls and firing holes, but did not neglect to have a lovely garden facing south to catch the best of the sun. He called this house Benholm's Lodgings. This may have referred to either his Mearns property or his childhood home, the Benholm's Lodgings that forms part of Dunnottar Castle.

Unfortunately, Sir Robert had little opportunity to enjoy his newly-acquired status, for he died in 1616 and his hard-won property was returned to his brother, the Earl Marischal. When the Earl died, Benholm's Lodgings was passed on to his doctor, followed by numerous other owners, and it remained a townhouse for many years. The building was bought by merchants, and in 1895, the basement and ground floor became licensed premises.

Many buildings had grown up beside the townhouse by this time, so its true pleasing architecture had become hidden. The surrounding streets were crowded and dirty, and just over the way stood a well, known as the 'wallie', so Benholm's Lodgings began to be referred to as the 'Wallie Hoose'. This name was gradually corrupted to become 'Wallace Tower', and confusion developed as to whether William Wallace had some association with the building.

Property developers began to regard the area as a prime retail site, and in the early 1960s, the land was bought by Lord Marks of Marks & Spencer. He had Benholm's Lodgings dismantled stone by stone and re-erected in Seaton Park, land previously owned by Sir Robert Keith himself. On the exterior of the Marks & Spencer building is a plaque indicating the site on which the town house used to stand.

In its current position, Benholm's Lodgings stands alone, and can be clearly appreciated, as it was when it was first built. When you visit, you can picture this fair town house in its former setting in the seventeenth century, alongside the green of St Katherine's Hill and wending cobbled streets leading down to the harbour.

Looking upon its walls, it is hard to see the detail of the Keith family crest with its motto *Veritas Vincit* (truth conquers), for weather and neglect have taken their toll. But it reminds me, as does the battered statue of the knight, of the impetuous young man who had Benholm's Lodgings built so many years ago.

The Astronomer from Aberdeen

Many prodigious inventors and scientists have emerged from this part of the world, not least David Gill, originally a student at Marischal College, Aberdeen. His story is not well known, but I hope this will change. – G.B.

'David! C'mon!' shouted Jemmie, 'it's late!'

'But Jem, look at that,' said David, gazing up at the sky in amazement, 'just bide a wee minute …'

'It's caul, Davie, an' it's three o'clock in the mornin'! Yer aye starin up at the stars!' said his brother in exasperation.

'Aye weel, it's amazin'.'

From a young age, David had constantly marvelled at nature; examining, testing and eager to explore new ideas. His chemistry teacher at Dollar Academy had done much to quicken his interest. At the Gills' home – No. 48 Skene Street, Aberdeen – the children converted one of the top rooms into a laboratory to which the brothers trailed back their treasures from the quarries for examination with dogged fascination.

David's boyhood enthusiasm for astronomy continued to grow. When he finished university, he wanted to set about making this hobby into a career. But his father regarded astronomy as just another pastime, alongside Davie's love for shooting and dancing. He had other ideas for his son's future.

'But Mr Maxwell said …'

'David, I ken how weel yer professor thinks on ye, but ye hiv a business tae run! My faither bigged up this clock business, an' as my eldest son, you hiv tae tak it forward!'

'Aye, faither, I ken.'

'Richt, weel, ye can ayewis hiv time in the gairden tae play aboot wi' yer astronomical instruments. It's good tae see ye wi' a hobby! But noo, ye'll be awa' tae London an Switzerland, then back tae England, an' by the time yiv finished yer trainin, I'll be almost ready tae retire!'

David smiled grimly towards his father. He had hoped to reason with him, but in his eyes, astronomy was not very lucrative, and was not to be considered as a career. Smarting from his father's response, David found his mother waiting anxiously in the next room.

'Weel, son?' David's mother looked at him hopefully, 'what did your father say?'

'No, of course, Mither.' David's voice was tight with frustration, but he knew his mother was worried. He smiled at her warmly. She had always been supportive of his inventions as a child, and knew just how much her Davie longed to throw himself into a career of astronomy. She believed he could do it.

'Never mind!' he said, 'I will learn ma clock trade weel, and as Faither said, I'll aye hiv ma ain instruments tae play wi'!'

When David left Marischal College in 1860 at the age of seventeen, he was well-equipped for much of what lay before him, through the guidance of two of his lecturers in particular. James Clerk Maxwell taught David natural philosophy, and engaged his mind in the consideration of that which surrounded him, incorporating many scientific disciplines, notwithstanding astronomy, providing David with skills of great value to him in years to come.

Dr David Rennett lectured in mathematics and natural philosophy also, enabling David to tackle almost any mathematical problem that he might encounter within his investigations.

Meantime, David directed his mind to work hard learning all he could about the watch-making trade. Although he felt the training would curb his fascination with science, the skills he acquired in working with the delicate mechanisations of clockwork would prove to be invaluable in the schemes and constructions he would develop in the future. By the time he had completed his training, he had even developed his own version of the marine chronometer.

Wherever David went, he made acquaintances, his character always pleasant and enthusiastic, and both abroad in Switzerland, and in Coventry and in Clerkenwell, he was received warmly.

When he returned to Aberdeen in 1863, his father proudly made him a junior partner in their shop at No. 78 Union Street, and there he might have remained but for his undying passion for the night sky. Having learned his trade well, David had become a respected man of knowledge and skill in clock design, and his ability encouraged him to experiment to see how the stars could assist in measuring time.

'Mr Thomson?'

'Is that you, David? Now … let me see … David … David Gill?'

'Aye, sir, it is! I didna expect ye tae remember me!'

'I rarely forget a face, and ye were ayewis so enthusiastic aboot the stars when we were up in the Cromwell Tower, and I seem tae recall ye didna mind me smoking ma pipe!' Both men laughed. 'It's been a few years since I've seen ye! So what's brocht ye back tae King's then?'

David's face lit up. 'Weel, sir …'

'Na, na, Davie's the name, jist Davie. I'm nae yer lecturer ony mair!'

'Weel then … Davie … I wis wonderin aboot that aul telescope … yiv never really used it, hiv ye?'

'No,' said Thomson, looking sheepish, 'I've never hid the inclination tae dee it.'

'Weel, sir, I hiv a grand idea! Wi' deein ma watchmaker's trainin, it occurs tae me tae see if we could set up the telescope tae observe the stars and get a readin o' true time, like Piazzi Smyth wi' his transit instrument an' his time gun that gangs aff in Edinburgh at one o'clock each day, ye ken?'

'In that case, I'd better get ye doon tae Smyth tae see how he's done it.'

When David returned, he was brimming over with ideas. '… aye, an' Piazzi let me inspect his instruments and the time gun. Weel, I think we could definitely dae the same wi' the telescope, an' connect it up tae a clock so abody in Aiberdeen will hiv accurate time, an' nae jist at one o'clock!'

'A' richt lad! The north dome in the Cromwell Tower, that's far we'll put it!'

It took some time for the two to set up the telescope, but David's enthusiasm was infectious, and soon a large number of folk at King's were involved in the project, from the sacrist to the students. They were taking measurements, hunting down ladders, while watching as David set about wiring up the clock on the turret to the telescope, using an electrical pendulum clock to drive it.

'Weel, David, is it accurate then?' asked Davie.

'Jist a minute! I hiv tae check wi' the telescope … ah! A wee adjustment tae make!'

'A'body's ootside, ye ken!'

'But it's three in the mornin'!'

'Aye, but yiv infected a'body wi' yon clock o' yours! Ye'll hiv tae gang doon an tell them the clock is richt!'

'Aye!' David said proudly. 'It'll be mair accurate than the cannon in Edinburgh noo!' He grinned.

The clock proved so popular that David decided to extend the wiring. 'I think we'll jist extend it tae Marischal College, gie them the benefit o' accurate time tae!' By this time, David had many students clamoring to be part of the project, and there was a great cheer.

'An' fit aboot tae Union Street sir? Tae yer clockmaking shop at number 78?' shouted one student cheekily.

'And why not indeed! Let's dae it!' laughed David.

The process was tricky, and some mistakes were made before they came up with a plan that worked, involving wooden poles, staggered along the length of the journey, to which wires were attached.

David's father watched his son make the finishing touches with a mixture of pride, amusement and exasperation. 'Ye ken yiv a shop tae run, David?'

'Aye, Faither, an' life tae enjoy!' He smiled, adjusting the wiring. 'That's it noo! Look! Come ootside!' His father hobbled out onto the street and looked up at the clock above the door, then at his son grinning boyishly down at him.

'There's nae stopping you lad, is there?'

He smiled and hobbled back indoors, half-shaking his head. He was pleased for David, as long as business did not suffer, and it was going well, he had to admit. But often, as now, he would feel uncertain of just where David's first love would take him.

'Davie?'

'Aye, David, I ken that tone a voice. Fit are ye thinking on noo?'

'Weel, I've heard there's anither telescope goin cheap, an equatorial een, an I thocht we could try an dae some trackin o the planets.'

'O richt! In the sooth dome, ye mean?'

'Aye!'

With this telescope, though not as accurate as David had hoped, the two were able to follow the movement of Mercury across the Sun in November, and then watch a solar eclipse in March 1887.

Not long after this achievement, David came running into the room where his mother was sitting, his eyes shining. 'Mither, I've bocht a'thin I need tae mak my ain telescope!' Bursting with the news, his mother smiled. Nothing changed with David – he was always discovering or creating, and always excited about something.

'That's wonderful, son! Noo yiv been talking aboot the moon to tak photographs o' – are ye goin tae dee that?' she asked, beaming at her son, delighted by his unfaded enthusiasm.

'I am!'

His mother listened patiently, nodding and laughing, bewildered and hardly grasping anything her son said, but caught up in his joy and passion.

So it was that David began to follow his dream, and when the opportunity finally arose, David chose to become a full-time astronomer, abandoning a life of security in the pursuit of science. His father was distressed that his son was no longer in the clock-making business, but David's wife, Isobel Black, whom he met and married in 1870 just before his mother died, was right behind his decision. With Isobel at his side, David Gill fulfilled his lifetime following a fascinating career which has placed him in the history books as a leading light in astronomy during the nineteenth century, whilst going on to become the Queen's Astronomer in South Africa.

Riddle Nine
My prints walk across the snow-white ground
Leaving my mark, my scent, my sound.

The Slave who came from Aboyne

This tale did not come from a storyteller, a relative, or a history book. Every twenty years or so, the gentlemen of the local Aberdeen press rediscover the tale of Indian Peter and run a feature on him. And the children love him! They draw him, they write plays about him, they act out his life story. And well they might, for Peter is one of the most colourful characters ever to come out of the North-East of Scotland. – S.B.

Peter Williamson was born in Hirnley, Aboyne in 1730. When he was eight, he was sent to stay with his aunt in Aberdeen, as his father, a poor crofter, could not earn enough money to feed the whole family. An adventurous little boy, he was soon to discover that curiosity killed the cat. One day, when he was thirteen, he wandered down to the quay to play with his friends. Being a sturdy, healthy child, he was spotted by two kidnappers who had come from a ship in the harbour.

They were paid by city merchants to steal children to sell as slaves in the American plantations. Many city magistrates, sea captains, and the town clerk deputy, Walter Cochran, were implicated in the scheme.

The children were kept locked up in a building opposite Aedie's House in the Green, and a piper was paid to drown out their screams. During the child-snatching days in Aberdeen, around 1,000 children were stolen off the streets to sell as slaves. Once the crew had enough to boys to fill their hold, usually around seventy, they would set sail for the New World. William, Peter's father, got wind of this, and as the children were being loaded onto the boat, he tried to rescue his son. William was severely beaten on the dockside, and Peter was dragged away.

The ship was called *The Planter*, skippered by Captain Robert Ragg, and the voyage across the Atlantic took eleven weeks. The ship was wrecked during a dreadful storm, approaching Cape May in Delaware, and the unfortunate boys were locked in the hold as the crew climbed into the only lifeboat and rowed safely ashore. The next day, the crew returned to find the ship intact and the children still alive, so they marched them to Philadelphia and sold them to anyone with money. It is thought 20 per cent perished in the crossing. Peter was lucky enough to be sold to a fellow Scot, Hugh Wilson, who had himself been press-ganged by the slavers when he was a child in St Johnstone. He set Peter to work on his farm all summer, but let him go to school in the winter to be educated.

After a few years, Hugh died, leaving his money, horse, clothes and saddle to Peter, who was now a free man. He travelled from place to place across America working as a labourer until he was twenty-four, when he fell in love and married a planter's daughter in Pennsylvania, being given a dowry of 200 acres of land.

The French and Indian War was raging, and nowhere was safe from attack. There came a time when his wife was away, leaving Peter alone in their cabin. The little homestead was attacked by Delaware Indians, who fired burning arrows into the roof to force him out. He was tied tightly to a tree whilst the Indians burned his feet. Fortunately, he did not shout out, and as a mark of respect for his bravery, he was allowed to live as a slave. His new captors used him as a pack horse.

During this time, they captured three Ulstermen from Cannocojigge, a small town near the river Susquehanna. A trader who fell into their hands was scalped and roasted alive, before being cannibalised, and his head turned into Indian pudding. The Ulstermen escaped but were recaptured, and two were disembowelled. The third was trussed like a hen, and buried upright with only his head above ground, whilst they lit fires around him and scalped him, condemning him to a slow death.

Some months after this, Peter managed to escape, having witnessed devilish tortures being inflicted on less fortunate settlers who were captured alive. By then, his wife had died. Broken-hearted, he joined a British colonial regiment to fight the French and their Indian allies, but he was captured once again, this time by the French near New York in 1756. For once, this was short lived, and he was traded in exchange for French prisoners, and shipped back to Britain for release. During these adventures, Peter had wounded a hand, and so was discharged from service with six shillings.

Like a homing pigeon, he was determined to return to Aberdeen. To raise the funds to get home, he wrote and published a book of his ordeals, called *French and Indian Cruelty: Exemplified in the Life and Various Vicissitudes of Fortune of Peter Williamson*, and then he dressed himself in Indian buckskins and feathers to perform their war dance, with whoops, war paint and a tomahawk. This always ensured an audience and good sales. Peter sold 1,000 copies, and in June 1758, he finally reached Aberdeen.

The general public of the city were appalled by his tale of child slavery. Local government officials and merchants brought him to trial for selling a book of a 'scurrilous and infamous libel'. His books were burned, and he was jailed until he signed a forced statement that his book was untrue. He also had to pay a ten shilling fine, before being released and banished from the town as a vagrant.

He travelled to Edinburgh and opened a coffee house, which became a popular meeting place for lawyers and hanging judges. His customers, learning of his ordeal, urged him to sue the magistrates of Aberdeen. The case was heard in the Court of Session and the first time round, merchants bribed the sheriff and made him drunk. The case was dismissed. Next time round, the sheriff was not to be bribed and Peter won his case. In 1763, Peter was awarded £200 in damages and 100 guineas cost.

After this, the tide of his fortunes really began to turn. He bought a tavern in Edinburgh in Old Parliament Close. The sign read: 'Peter Williamson, vintner from the other world'. In 1773, he compiled Auld Reekie's first street directory. Three years later, he launched a weekly paper called *The Scots Spy or Critical Observer*, full of articles about contemporary matters and local gossip. Not content with this, he started a penny post and had letters and packages delivered. In 1793, The Williamson Penny Post joined

the general post office, and Peter was given a handsome pension. In 1799, after a very eventful life, Peter Williamson of Hirnley, Aboyne, died and was buried in Old Calton Cemetery, Edinburgh.

Not only did his life inspire James Fenimore Cooper to write *The Last of the Mohicans*, but also it is said to be the basis of the film *A Man Called Horse*.

Alexander Hadden of Hadden Mill

The Green is a fascinating area in Aberdeen, steeped in a wealth of history. This was the original highway into the city centre. The main thoroughfare was down Windmill Brae, and over the Denburn by the Bow Brig to enter the Green. This led on to the Netherkirkgate and then up to the Castlegate. The King's palace was situated down in this area back in the thirteenth century.

I researched the following account and discovered that Hadden's Mill had used the Denburn as its water source, and was sited where the Trinity car park now stands. – G.B.

There once was a young Aberdonian whose name was Alexander Hadden. He was born in 1720 and lived in Windmill Brae. Alexander was a spirited lad, and was keen to find his own way into business. But after various trials, every door seemed closed in the city, so he decided to leave and seek his fortune elsewhere.

One morning, he set out with his staff and bundle. When he reached the Bridge of Dee, however, and found himself in a place that was strange and unfamiliar, his resolve wavered. Doubtful whether to continue or return home, he decided to throw his staff as far as he could and whichever way it landed, that would be the way he would travel. He threw the stick ahead of him with all his might and watched as it sailed through the sky and landed flat on the ground. He ran up to it and found that the point was facing back the way he had just come.

With a heavy heart, Alexander retraced his steps and returned to the Green. He felt quite silly and thought his neighbours would mock him. But one woman, hearing his tale, quietly approached him and said, 'Alec, you're a fiery young man. I would like to give you a chance to make your own way in life. Here.' She handed him a five pound note. Alexander looked at her in astonishment. 'I canna tak that!'

'Aye ye can! You want your own business, do you nae?'

'Aye,' said Alexander, nodding.

'Weel next Friday, I want ye at the Green merket early, no lyin a' bed! Ye hiv tae catch a' the country wifies as they arrive wi' their hose that they've been makin for the toonsers. They're verra popular, ye ken! Yer tae buy them a' wi' this money, and then ye can set up a stall in the merket an sell them on for a profit!'

Alexander grinned broadly. He was delighted with the idea. 'I will! Ye wilna regret this!' 'An' mind!' said the woman smiling, 'I wint ma money back wi' interest!'

The following Friday, Alexander rose at what he thought was a decent hour. Rubbing his eyes, he made his way to the market in the Green, and found it bustling, though there was no sign of the country wifies with their hose. But then he noticed a stall already set up, covered in colourful stockings, with Baillie Dingwall shouting out his wares to passers-by. Frustrated but not discouraged, Alexander made sure that the following Friday it was Baillie Dingwall who arrived at his usual time to find a young man making good trade in hose.

This was Alexander Hadden's breakthrough, and from these small beginnings, he started to see how he could grow his enterprise. He sought a way to supply quality raw material to the cottar women, for them to knit stockings in their own homes and return the finished articles at an agreed price.

As business began to expand, Hadden decided more profit could be made from having his own machines in town, so he opened his own woollen mill, Hadden Mill, in the Green. It had been a mill site since the 1750s, and was previously the Carmelite Friars' kiln. The mill gradually developed to specialise in spinning and weaving, and by the late nineteenth century, it was one of the largest carpet manufacturers in Britain, with additional mills

at Garlogie (1832) and Gordon Mills (1875), which supplied the material for making the carpets.

Bailie Dingwall's daughter married Alexander, and this was the origin of three generations of powerful businessmen who, through intermarriage, were one of the most influential families in Aberdeen, influencing politics and dealings in the city for many years.

WEE AIPPLIES AN' WEE ORANGIES

When Stanley Robertson told me this tale, he said that it came from the very poorest part of Aberdeen. As Stanley didn't specify the exact location, I've set this version in Ghaist's Raw, near the Castlegate. At one time this was a notorious slum area. Here, prostitutes lived who propositioned the soldiers from the Castlehill barracks, and the rough seamen from the city docks. The narrow wynds and lanes were verminous, filthy, stinking, and rife with disease. Up to sixteen people lived in one house, often many more. Ghaist's Raw ran parallel to Broad Street and was known from early times as 'the street of spirits' because it overlooked St Nicholas kirkyard. Tales of ghosts and supernatural sightings have long been linked to the area. To add to its unsavoury reputation, it was noted for the activities of bodysnatchers. The travelling people had an inbuilt fear of being dragged from the streets by burkers (doctors) or noddies (medical students) and thereafter carted to the nearby anatomy theatre and butchered by the anatomists. Stanley described the burkers as having a coach, draped in a black cloth with a zinc floor punctured with holes to allow the blood of murdered victims to drip out freely. The horses' hooves were muffled by rubber pads, and the burkers and noddies were dressed in the clothes of undertakers. – S.B.

If you visit Aberdeen today, you may find yourself standing beside a magnificent statue of King Robert the Bruce on horseback, holding up his charter to the city, against the glorious glittering backdrop of Marischal College, with its granite spires soaring up

to the sky. But if you had visited Aberdeen long ago, this street was less than splendid, facing as it did, Ghaist's Raw – the street of the ghosts. Here lay a warren of the worst slums in the city, with families packed in like herring in a creel. Working families, mind you, not beggars nor vagrants, for they found shelter in the workhouse or the tender ministrations of the model lodging house, where dozens of the unwashed poor slept on the floor for a token fee per night.

Two families lived in a cramped tenement in this insanitary crannie of poverty, in two separate bedsits, each housing a couple with a single child apiece, both girls, who went by the names of Wee Aipplies and Wee Orangies. Wee Aipplies was named for her rosy cheeks, red as apples. Wee Orangies was named for her good Scots hair, that fair-gold-reddish hair of the ancient Celts that a Faerie Queen would be proud of. Her real name was Jeannie, but only Wee Aipplies called her that. Not only were the two girls neighbours, they were the best of friends; inseparable, in fact. On washdays, Wee Aipplies would lift the dripping clothes from the washtub out in the yard and Wee Orangies would feed them through the mangle, cranking as fast as her skinny little arms could manage.

Things went reasonably well for a while with the two families. Both fathers had work nearby, Wee Aipplies' father as a blacksmith, and Wee Orangies' father as a porter down at the harbour, unloading heavy crates of tea and other goods, coming off the clippers home from the Far East. Then, one bitter stormy day in October, Wee Aipplies' mother came home soaked to the skin. Two days later, she started to cough. They tried the usual remedies – hot salt in a woollen sock laid on her throat, toddy and honey – but years of hard work and a poor diet had left her too weak to fight off infection. Within the month she was dead. Determined that she could at least have a decent burial, her grieving husband spent the little savings he had on a coffin and a grave, though he could not afford a headstone and instead forged a metal heart from a horseshoe with her name on it. This, he hammered into the site as a marker.

Death had not completed his work in that sombre tenement, however, for almost to the day that Wee Aipplies' mother was buried, an apprentice shipwright ran panting up the brae from the harbour to Ghaist's Raw with news that Wee Orangies' father had been killed. He had died outright when a rope snapped, swinging a huge chest of tea from ship to shore. The unfortunate man was the son of a ship's mate, and knowing how poor the family were, some of the local seamen agreed to row the body out over the harbour bar, and give him a sea burial. Many of those who lived in Ghaist's Raw could not scrape together the money needed for burying a loved one ... dead children were often kept in the house in a cupboard drawer, till the cost of a basic funeral could be met.

This left Wee Aipplies motherless, and Wee Orangies without a father as a breadwinner. Wee Aipples father tried in vain to find a woman to care for his little girl to leave him free to work, but with wages so meagre, he could find no one who was suitable. It was too dangerous to have Wee Aipples with him around the forge. 'Why don't you marry the widow next door?' a customer suggested. 'After all, she's just lost her husband and the two girls are friends. It could solve both your problems.'

And so, Wee Aipples gained a stepmother, and Wee Orangies became her sister. But a stepmother does not always show love towards another woman's child. The stepmother was jealous of Wee Aipples' beauty and popularity, though she was careful not to show it. She was always perfect and kind in her dealings with the little girl in front of her new husband, but when he was out at work, it was a different tale altogether. There wasn't a dirty, wearisome job in the house, but Wee Aipples was made to do it. For reward she was given a kick or a curse. The clothes her mother had painstakingly sewn for her out of love were pawned for gin by the stepmother. Nobody combed out her curls, or hugged her when she was sad; only Wee Orangies tried to make the life of her friend more bearable, though she, too, was scared of her mother's temper.

One day, the stepmother was baking scones, when she ran out of milk. Down below in the street could be heard the clatter of the milkman's horse's hooves striking the flinty cobbles. The wicked woman took down a big glass jug, and handed it to Wee Aipplies, with a silver threepenny.

'Go down the stairs and get him to fill this jug. And mind, if you break this jug, you useless baggage, I'll kill you stone dead, for that jug's a favourite of mine, worth ten of you.'

Poor Wee Aipplies ran downstairs to catch up with the milkman, but just as she reached the tail of the cart, she slid on a patch of wet straw and the jug went flying, crashing down on the road and shattering into a million pieces. Such was her terror of her stepmother's rage that she sobbed inconsolably into her petticoats. The milkman was a kind man, with children of his own.

'There, there wee lassie,' he said. 'It's only an old jug, and not the bonniest, either. It's not worth tuppence that I can see. Here, I'll give you this jug for nothing, it's twice the jug that old one was,' and he filled the new jug up to the brim.

But Wee Aipplies knew better, she knew how cruel her stepmother could be and how easy it was to spark her anger. Fearfully, she crept up the stairs, and set the jug down on the table. The woman's eyes narrowed.

'What's this? What's this? This isn't the jug I gave you! I'll teach you to try to cheat me, you wee rogue!' and quick as a flash, she unhooked a heavy pan hanging above the fire and flung it full force at the terrified girl.

The metal pan hit Wee Aipplies full force on the brow, and she dropped like a stone to the floor.

'Mother, mother, what have you done?' cried Wee Orangies in alarm, bending to tend to her friend.

'She's fakin it, she's fakin it,' cried the wicked woman. And she gave Wee Orangies money and sent her quite to the other side of town for a box of snuff, knowing she'd be away until teatime.

That night, Wee Orangies and her stepfather arrived at the tenement stairs together.

'Where's your sister?' he cried laughing, and tossed her up in the air.

'She fell, stepfather,' the little girl replied, not daring to add that her mother had struck Wee Aipplies.

Inside the room was filled with an appetising smell of stew. The table was beautifully laid, with four places set, the huge stewpot down in the middle, with the large black ladle beside it. The stepmother rubbed the bowls on her apron till they gleamed, and told her husband and her daughter to help themselves.

'Shouldn't we wait for Wee Aipplies?' the man asked.

'She's already had something,' said the woman. 'I let her out to play before bedtime.'

Was there ever a stew as rich, and sweet and fine as the one that was eaten that night? One helping, two helpings, three each, and the pot was down to the scrapings. The man was just tipping the last dregs into his bowl, when he heard a chink ... and looking down, to his amazement, he saw his Wee Aipplies' green stone ring lying there, winking up at him. Now, the game was up! The stepmother had to confess that in her rage she had killed Wee Aipplies, and cooked her flesh in the pot.

'What was I to do?' she wailed. 'It was an accident. And who would look after Wee Orangies and yourself if the police were to take me away? And how would we have paid for a funeral, and us too poor to sole our boots?'

By lies and tears she made her husband think that the death was a dreadful mistake. But late that night Wee Orangies raked through the fire where the bones of her sister had been thrown, gathered them up in a pail, and walked on her little bare feet to the pauper's cemetery, where she covered them up with a cairn of stones. If you could have watched over that cairn of stones, later that night when the stars were sharp with frost, you would have seen the ghost of a tiny dove rise up from the cemetery, for the God who watches the innocents loved Wee Aipplies, and turned her into a bird to join him in Heaven.

Soon it was the Christmas Season. Up in Heaven, Wee Aipplies grew restive looking down on Earth, and itched to be part of that time of giving and grace. She asked St Peter's permission to visit the land of mortals, and he tugged his grizzled beard and agreed. He also granted her the gift of speech, in her form of a heavenly dove. Down she floated, down, down, down on a snow cloud, into the dark streets of her old home in Aberdeen. She came to rest on the window ledge of a dollmaker's house; his glasses perched on the end of his nose, he tapped tiny tacks into the wooden limbs of a doll. Up and down the snowy window ledge she paraded, tapping the glass pane with her beak. The dollmaker set aside his work, and glanced up.

'Bless me and save me,' he said, 'if it isn't a wee dove. I wonder what it wants. Maybe it's hungry?'

And he opened the window to toss out some crumbs. To his surprise, the wee dove opened its beak and spoke.

'Dollmaker,' she cooed. 'Would you make me a wee doll for a Christmas present?'

Once the dollmaker recovered from his surprise that a dove could speak, he asked what she could give him as payment for the present.

'I can sing you a song,' replied Wee Aipplies, and she opened her beak and began:

My mammy killed me
My daddy ate me
My sister Jeannie buried my bones
And covered me up with the graveyard stones
And I flew and I grew
Tae a bonnie wee doo-oo.

'What a strange song,' said the dollmaker. But he handed over the present, and the dove lifted it onto her cloud of snow, and floated back to Heaven again.

Next day, back she went to St Peter, with the same request as before. Again, it was granted. But this time, when Wee Aipplies flew to Earth, she came to rest on the window ledge of a watchmaker. The watchmaker was deftly sifting through tiny gold cogs and wheels and broken bits of machinery, fitting them into the back of gentleman's fob watch. Up and down the snowy window ledge she paraded, tapping the glass pane with her beak. The watchmaker set aside his work, and glanced up.

'Bless me and save me,' he said, 'if it isn't a wee dove. I wonder what it wants. Maybe it's hungry?'

And he opened the window to toss out some crumbs. To his surprise, the wee dove opened its beak and spoke.

'Watchmaker,' she cooed. 'Would you make me a watch for a Christmas present?'

Once the watchmaker recovered from his surprise that she could speak, he asked what she could give him as payment for the present.

'I can sing you a song,' replied Wee Aipplies, and she opened her beak and began:

> My mammy killed me
> My daddy ate me
> My sister Jeannie buried my bones
> And covered me up with the graveyard stones
> And I flew and I grew
> Tae a bonnie wee doo-oo.

'What a strange song,' said the watchmaker. But he handed over the present, and the dove lifted it onto her cloud of snow, and floated back to Heaven again.

Next day, back she went to St Peter, with the same request as twice before. Again, it was granted. But this time, when Wee Aipplies flew to Earth, she came to rest on the window ledge of her father's own smithy, where he pointed a horse's shoes, sharpening them to keep their grip on the icy roads. Up and down the snowy window ledge she paraded, tapping the glass pane with her beak. Her father set aside his work, and glanced up.

'Bless me and save me,' he said, 'if it isn't a wee dove. I wonder what it wants. Maybe it's hungry?'

And he set down his blacksmith's hammer, and opened the window to toss out some crumbs. To his surprise, the wee dove opened its beak and spoke.

'Blacksmith,' she cooed. 'Would you make me a knife for a Christmas present?'

Once the blacksmith recovered from his surprise that the dove could speak, he asked what she could give him as payment for the present.

'I can sing you a song,' replied Wee Aipplies, for the final time, and she opened her beak and began:

> My mammy killed me
> My daddy ate me
> My sister Jeannie buried my bones
> And covered me up with the graveyard stones
> And I flew and I grew
> Tae a bonnie wee doo-oo.

'What a sad, strange song,' said the blacksmith. But he handed over the present, and the dove lifted it onto her cloud of snow, and floated back to Heaven again.

Next day was Christmas Day. St Peter allowed Wee Aipplies to return to Earth for a last visit. The little bird had presents to deliver. In the smoky, cramped bedsit that was her old home, her stepmother, father and stepsister were seated at their Christmas meal. Just as her father was about to carve a slice from the goose's breast, there came a sound from the chimney. A high-pitched sound, like that of a young girl, echoed around the room.

'Daddy! Daddy!' came the voice. 'Would you like a present from your Wee Aipplies?'

The family looked on in surprise, as a small parcel floated down from the chimney as if by magic and landed with a thump by her father's plate.

'My goodness!' called her father, opening the parcel and finding the watch. 'This is a gift from my Wee Aipplies!'

'Orangies! Orangies!' came the voice. 'Would you like a present from your Wee Aipplies?'

Again the family looked on in surprise, as a second small parcel floated down from the chimney as if by magic and landed with a thump, this time by Wee Orangies' plate.

'My goodness!' called her father, as his stepdaughter opened the parcel and found the beautiful doll. 'Another gift from my Wee Aipplies!'

'Nothing for me, though, selfish, selfish, selfish to the end,' muttered her stepmother. 'Stepmother! Stepmother!' came the voice. 'Would you like a present from your Wee Aipplies?'

The stepmother rushed towards the chimney and looked up. The last thing she saw was a beautiful little knife, ever so sharp, flying out of the dark, which cut her up into a thousand and one pieces, as small as silver threepennies.

Her work done, Wee Aipplies floated up to Heaven and was never seen on Earth again.

Riddle Ten
You leave never to return
I knew you
But did not know it

RIDDLES SOLVED

Riddle One
A river

Riddle Two
Imagination tickled by a tale

Riddle Three
Pussywillow

Riddle Four
A raindrop

Riddle Five
Elder tree

Riddle Six
My shadow

Riddle Seven
A ring

Riddle Eight
The eye

Riddle Nine
A writer

Riddle Ten
A breath

BIBLIOGRAPHY

Primary Sources

Isobel Craib (Hill o' Fare & Corrichie)
Nancy Mackintosh
Charles Middleton Ritchie (Ballater Legends)
Helen Mochrie
Lizzie Philip (Skene and Tarland Legends)
Stanley Robertson
Helen Strachan
John Watt Stewart (City & Lower Deeside legends)
Les Wheeler (Braemar Legends)

Secondary Sources

Blelack
Farquharson, D.R., *Tales & Memories of Cromar and Canada*
   (Ontario, 1900)

Auld Slorachs
Watson, A., & Allan, E. (Aberdeen: AUP, 1984)

Knock Castle
Mitchie, G., *Deeside Tales: or Men Manners on Highland Deeside
   since 1745* (Aberdeen: Wyllie & son, 1908)

The Strange Coachman
The New Statistical Account of Scotland Volume XII (Aberdeen
    United Parishes of Glenmuick, Tullich and Glengairn, 1845)

The Tattiebogle
McNeill, F. Marian, *The Silver Bough* (Edinburgh: Canongate
    Books Ltd, 2001)

Templar Thunder Hole
Aitken, Robert, 'The Knights Templar in Scotland', *The Scottish
    Review* (July 1898)

The Rat, the Tree and the Dragon
Gordon, S., *The Cairngorm Hills Of Scotland* (London: Cassell &
    Co, 1925)
Grant, J., *Legends of the Braes o' Mar* (Aberdeen, 1861)
MacDonald, J., *Place Names in Strathbogie* pp.258–259 (Dwyllie
    & Son, 1891)

French Kate
Wyness, F., *More Spots from the Leopard* (Impulse Books, 1973)

Alison Cross
Child, F.J., *The English and Scottish Popular Ballads, Vol.1*,
    pp.313–4 (New York: Dover Publications, 1965)

The Plague Castle
McConnochie, A.I., & Murray, J.D., *The Royal Dee: A Description
    of the River from the Wells to the Sea* (Scotland: Jolly Publishers
    1898)

The Smith of Kildrummy Castle
Tabraham, C.J., *Historic Buildings and Monuments* (The Stationery
    Office, 1986)

The Children of the Trough
Scott, Walter, Sir, *Tales of a Grandfather; Being Stories Taken from Scottish History* (Edinburgh: A & C Black, 1889)

The Tad Losgann
Wyness, F., *Legends of North-East Scotland: Stories for the Young and not so Young* (Gramercy Pub. Co, 1970)

The Laird o' Drum
Child Ballad 263A

The Key Pool
MacQuarrie, Alan, 'Scottish Saints' Legends in the Aberdeen Breviary', in Boardman, Steve, and Williamson, Eila (eds.), *The Cult of Saints and the Virgin Mary in Medieval Scotland (Studies in Celtic History 28)* (Woodbridge: Boydell Press, 2010)

The Wizard Laird o' Skene
McPherson, J.M., *Primitive Beliefs in the North-East of Scotland* (Kessinger Publishing Co, 2003)

Reel o' Tulloch
Grant, J., *Legends of the Braes o' Mar* (Aberdeen, 1861)
Wyness, F., *Legends of North-East Scotland: Stories for the Young and not so Young* (Gramercy Pub. Co, 1970)

The Slave who came from Aboyne
Skelton, D., *Indian Peter: The Extraordinary Life and Adventures of Peter Williamson* (Random House, 2012)

Wee Aipplies and Wee Orangies
Graham, C., *Portrait of Aberdeen and Deeside* (London: Robert Hale, 1980)

Anderson, Robert, *Aberdeen in Bygone Days* (*Aberdeen Daily Journal*, 1910)

Cluer, Andrew, & Winram, Andrew, *Walkin' the Mat: Past Impressions of Aberdeen* (Winram-Cluer, 1975)

Forbes, G., *Sir David Gill* (Book on Demand, 1916)

Fraser, W.H. & Lee, C.H., *Aberdeen 1800–2000: A New History* (Tuckwell Press Ltd., 2000)

Keith, Alexander, *A Thousand Years of Aberdeen* (Mercat Press, 1980)

Morgan, Diane, *Lost Aberdeen* (Birlinn Ltd., 2004)

Riordan, James, *The Woman in the Moon* (Hutchinson, 1984)

Wyness, F., *City by the Grey North Sea – Aberdeen* (Alex P. Reid & Sons, 1966)

ONLINE SOURCES

http://www.archive.org/stream/davidgillmanastr00forbrich/davidgillmanastr00forbrich_djvu.txt http://homepages.abdn.ac.uk/nph120/astro/cto/

http://www.egcp.org.uk/coast/folksofforvie.php

http://www.kittybrewster.com/ancestry/keith.htm http://mcjazz.f2s.com/Textiles.htm

http://www.mcjazz.f2s.com/Smuggling.htm

http://mcjazz.f2s.com/14thCentWaterSupply.htm

http://www.scottish-places.info/features/featurefirst8959.html

http://www.scottish-places.info/towns/townhistory617.html

http://sites.scran.ac.uk/collieston/Century/1800/Stories.html

If you enjoyed this book, you may also be interested in …

Highland Folk Tales
Bob Pegg

The Highlands of Scotland are rich in traditional stories. They are tales of the sidh – the fairy people – and their homes in the green hills; of great and gory battles, and of encounters with the last wolves in Britain; of solitary ghosts, and of supernatural creatures like the sinister waterhorse, the mermaid, and the Fuath, Scotland's own Bigfoot.

978 0 7524 6090 1

Derbyshire Folk Tales
Pete Castle

Passed down from generation to generation, many of Derbyshire's most popular folk tales are gathered together here for the first time. Ranging from stories specific to the region, such as 'The Derby Ram', to others which are local versions of well-known classics, like 'Beauty and the Beast', all of the tales in this collection are rooted in Derbyshire's past.

978 0 7524 5388 0

Visit our website and discover thousands of other History Press books.

www.thehistorypress.co.uk

Lightning Source UK Ltd.
Milton Keynes UK
UKOW03f1449040914

238062UK00002B/3/P